Our Home of *Love*

From a Dog's Perspective

ANITA NEAL

ISBN 978-1-0980-0273-2 (paperback)
ISBN 978-1-0980-0274-9 (digital)

Copyright © 2019 by Anita Neal

All rights reserved. No part of this publication may be reproduced, distributed, or transmitted in any form or by any means, including photocopying, recording, or other electronic or mechanical methods without the prior written permission of the publisher. For permission requests, solicit the publisher via the address below.

Christian Faith Publishing, Inc.
832 Park Avenue
Meadville, PA 16335
www.christianfaithpublishing.com

Printed in the United States of America

The Quest

The companionship from a dog shows a pure form of love and devotion to its caretaker. When that companion departs from us, we can feel the severity of that loss only to acquire another—not to replace the companion we lost but to strengthen us and to expand that love we had been shown. May we always be deserving of that devotion.

Prologue

Junior stood up trying to regain his balance as he was being engulfed by a deep fog. His vision was poor, but he had been used to that since he was blind in one eye since birth. He had been deaf since birth as well, so he was not sure what this eerie whisper sound was where it felt like he was hearing.

"Hello, Junior."

Junior's head snapped to attention as now he knew he was actually hearing and hearing well for the first time. He also recognized the voice.

"Master," he acknowledged.

"Do you want me to call you Junior or Dittims?"

"Well, my given name was Junior, but I think the loving nickname of Dittims is what I would prefer if that's okay with you?"

"I prefer Dittims as well, but I wanted you to be comfortable with the choice."

The voice was coming from the center of the bright iridescent fog as it surrounded him.

"Where am I?"

"You are home."

"My home?" Junior said, puzzled, never remembering fog this thick.

"Yes. And mine."

"Yours," Dittims whispered, trying to distinguish a body in the billowing fog. "That means…"

"Yes, it does," God tenderly spoke.

"But I never expected to be able to come here."

"Yes, I know. But you were a good and faithful companion for your caretaker, and I still have much work for you to do to further my plans. Do you think you are up for the task?"

"Yes, sure, I will help you in any way that I can. I just may not be able to help as efficiently as others would. What is it that I can do for you?"

"I first need you to connect with your Love Team. They are waiting for you. They will get you acclimated to your surroundings and help show you how things are done here. Learn from them. Learn who they are and what they believe your capabilities are. You have much to learn here with your new abilities, and once you get settled, I will give you further task to help us all prepare for the strength of character that I know you possess. It will be much needed for my purposes later."

"Okay," said Dittims somewhat warily as he looked around seeing the fog slowly dissipate.

"Follow the path on your left down to the plateau, and there will be someone there to guide you further. I will see you off and on as you learn deeper of my ways."

Dittims turned to head down path but stopped momentarily, turned back, and gazed at the brightness of the light. "Again, thank you. I will give you all that my abilities will allow me to do."

"I have no doubt of that."

Chapter 1

> In my Father's house are many rooms... I
> am going there to prepare a place for you.
> —John 14:2 (NIV)

Dittims continued along the path as directed. The thickness of the fog slowly turned to a clear brightness he had never known. The pull he felt was leading him to a high-suspension bridge that crossed over an impressive set of falls. Beneath the falls were ragged cliffs that dropped steadily downward to where the falls crashed into the small clear lake. The water then cascaded down a smaller set of falls before creating a wide river running through the forest. The mist from the waterfalls combined with the brightness of light placed an ever-shimmering rainbow over the bridge. He stopped on the bridge and took in the beauty of everything around him, realizing the full gift of sight. Eagles were soaring in the wind currents above him, and many other birds were nested in the nooks and crannies down the length of rock wall.

Dittims looked across the bridge and saw the large marble plateau he had been told about. It was oval in shape, and in its center was a massive heart-shaped fountain with the word *agape* etched across its face. The water came up out of the center of the heart going up through the three intertwining clear tubes that also had words etched on them. Etched on one was *truth*, on another was *mercy*, and on the last and largest tube was *grace*. As the water overflowed the tops of these tubes, it cascaded down through several levels of glistening troughs where they emptied into a clear pool before plunging over the plateau's edge, creating the spectacular waterfall. There were benches surrounding the fountain where you could sit and watch the water and chat with friends as several groups seemed to be doing.

Far beyond the plateau was what seemed to be an impressive city where a brilliant light illuminated everything you could see. The center of the light was intense but comforting to look at, and its outer edges seemed to reflect various shades of green that Dittims had never seen before.

Coming out of the city was another river that flowed down into the valley beyond the city, then disappeared behind tall evergreen trees of a rolling forest that stretched for miles.

Dittims continued on across the bridge and stepped down onto a graveled path. He noticed that the path had beautiful lightly fragrant lilies on either side as it led to a desk just in front of the fountain. Behind the desk stood a tall slender gentleman in a glistening white uniform that beckoned him forward. Next to the gentleman stood a large vibrant white German shepherd that was patiently waiting on Junior's approach.

"Welcome, Dittims," said the gentleman reviewing his clipboard. "If you will head this way, Sasha and I will give you brief directions to help you get started on this leg of your journey."

As Dittims moved forward, the gentleman continued, "You will not need much guidance as your spirit knows where you are going. You are now at your true home. We all have an internal homing beacon. This beacon draws us toward our final destination where our loved ones and old friends who got here ahead of us are now waiting for our arrival."

"In your case," explained Sasha, the white German shepherd, "your caretaker has not arrived yet, so other members of your Love Team are waiting on your arrival."

"Yes, I was told about a Love Team but not sure what that means," said Dittims.

OUR HOME OF LOVE

"In homes where pets were loved," she explained, "those loved pets work together in unity as a Love Team."

"Sasha," said the gentleman, "if you will please take Dittims over to the arbor and pathway for Sector 19 and help him get started for his new life here."

As the gentleman turned back to Dittims, he said, "Sasha, will show you where to start and answer any questions you may have."

"Thank you," Dittims spoke softly as he was patted lovingly on the back.

As they moved toward Sector 19, Dittims took in the vast size of the plateau and saw several arbors with their own path spaced all around the oval. Each arbor was numbered, and they all looked similar in shape but were distinct with their individual displays of different flowers hanging through the latticed openings of each arbor. Sector 19 had large gardenia bushes on either side of the arbor opening with so many blooms on the bushes you could barely see the leaves. Intertwined through the openings of the lattice work overhead were tiny tea roses of a rich velvety-red color whose fragrance mixed and mingled with the gardenias, making you want to just stand there and breathe in the sweet air around you.

"Welcome to Sector 19," said Sasha as they stopped near the entrance to where Dittims would begin his journey. "Wow, you are a big guy," she teased him as she saw him tower over her.

"Yes," he replied. "I am a Harlequin Great Dane. But my coloring is mostly white like you. I just have this one black spot on my right side in the shape of a heart, which I always thought was special. Although," Dittims thought for a moment, "your white is really white. I'm sorry, but I can't think of a better way to describe it."

Sasha laughed. "So is your white. Have you not noticed?"

Dittims reviewed himself more thoroughly. "When I first got here, I noticed for the first time I could hear, but I didn't notice until just now how clearly I could see. So, no, I did not notice my white was bright as well."

"Yes," she said as she dipped in a mock bow. "It's our new look. Our dead seed has been dropped in God's wonderful soil, covered to regrow new life, and now we have become a brighter version of his beautiful creation."

"Sorry," said Dittims, "I don't understand."

"Did you ever see your caretaker plant seeds, and then a week later, a beautiful new plant would start to grow?" she asked.

"There was some of that, but I really didn't pay attention."

"It is a similar parallel for us here, and it is spoken about in the scriptures. Our earthly bodies have died and are being transformed by God into a more beautiful version of what we once were."

"Hmm," said Dittims as he pondered this new information.

"As we begin our journey here," continued Sasha, "we begin to understand better what our individual traits and characteristics are and how to better use them for the glory of…here. We all reflect the love and glory of the Master and share those individual gifts that were given to us that make us unique"—they looked around at their surroundings—"to complete his ultimate plan.

"There are many special and beautiful things to see here, and the more you see, the more there is to see. Also the more you see, the more you will understand his love. The more you understand his love, the more you will know what your individual gifts and traits are. Then you will understand what he needs you to do to help him with his plan.

"You will be looking for District 51 and street number 9. Once you get going, your senses will kick in and lead you right to your home. The house number you are looking for is 904-TC4. Enjoy your walk, and begin to enjoy the many facets of love and joy that are here. Do you have any questions for me at this time?"

Dittims looked around the large oval noticing again the arbors numbered from 20 down to 1, and then there was a gate that was all the way to the opposite side of the oval that had a white picket fence labeled as "Before." That gate and its path led up to a higher plateau. Although he could not see it clearly, there seemed to be arbors around it as well. He could also see a different path coming down from the mountain similar to the path that he had just come down himself. Dittims felt a couple of people coming up behind, and not wanting to be in their way, he stepped to the side to let them pass through the arbor.

"Yes, I do have a few," said Dittims. "My first question is, how are we able to communicate with people using words and we can understand one another? Sometimes, we don't even have to speak. Like just now, as that man just walked up behind me, he said, 'Excuse me,' but I didn't hear it with my ears. I sort of felt it."

"Well, do you remember your caretaker reading the stories from God's Word? And especially how in Revelation 4, how all the people and angels, as well as all the creatures spoke and worshiped God?"

"Yes, I do. I just didn't think about that." He softly spoke as he remembered the many readings they had enjoyed together.

"There were other stories as well like in Numbers 22, where a donkey spoke to Balaam because he was being mistreated. God has always intended for a partnership between all members of his creation."

"I guess that makes sense. The next question I have is about that fountain. As I came across the bridge, I noticed words carved into it in various places. I assume those words mean something. Can you explain those to me?"

"Yes. The word on the heart represents one of the five types of love created by God. Agape is God's love. It is unconditional love. It is the type of love that knows no bounds. It is carved on the fountain, so that is the first thing you see coming across the bridge. It's a reminder to all of creation that we never left his heart. And the other words reflect the Master himself in showing all the ways he has worked to assure that all of creation would be with him…forever."

Dittims thought on that for a long moment before asking his last question. "I guess I am just curious as to how all this works and the purpose for the different sectors.

"Well, we are all part of God's plan. He created all things, and each creation has a purpose, some short and some long, according to his will. And you and I are all part of the animal kingdom like first created in Eden. The different sectors are just a way of dividing time. They represent a beginning point for given time, and each sector has both man and beast as the Master created both to fulfill his purpose.

As stated in Psalm 50, every animal of the forest, every beast on a thousand hills, and all the creatures of the field are his. And man, according to Genesis, was created according to his likeness, so we all have a purpose in our creation and an appointed time of being.

"I remember Christy reading aloud often from the Bible," said Dittims. "I especially loved the comfort of the psalms and of course the wonderful and amazing stories throughout. I am also very fond of the stories in Genesis, like the telling of creation. Then there is Noah and the flood and the tower of Babel. And there is the explanation about different tribes of God's people and the kings, then Jesus and, well, all of it really."

"Yes, they are all favorites to us here. You were fortunate to have a person that read out loud so that you also could hear the teachings about the Bible. But there is a lot more to understanding of his ways here to help us get where we need to be to fulfill his plan. You will eventually understand all of that and his purpose for you as well. Then you will be able to move around and explore any of the sectors as desired. You have a strong Love Team, and they will help you get started in your learning."

Dittims nodded an affirmation even though he really did not fully understand her explanation, but seeing that she was turning back to the desk, he thought he would figure it out soon enough. There were others coming off the bridge that evidently needed her and the gentleman's attention. He looked around the large oval once more before turning and heading through the arbor marked for Sector 19.

Chapter 2

Home, a place where we are loved
and can love others freely.

Sector 19, District 51, Street 9, 904-TC4

The grass was green and lush around him as he continued down the walk at an easy pace being drawn toward his final home. Large oak trees periodically lined either side of the roadway, and lilies of various colors surrounded each trunk. The air smelled fresh and clean like it had recently rained, but there was no moisture on the ground.

Once through the arbor, the different district locations of each sector were easy to follow as they were numbered from 1 and going up. The districts were located on the left-hand side of the road with beautiful grassy fields located on the right-hand side. Patches of Queen Anne's lace, daisies, and cosmos gave the grassy areas a warm happy look. As Junior rounded a curve, he saw a familiar face heading his way.

"Lakota," he shouted excitedly. "Hey, how are you?"

"Junior, it's good to see you. Are you just now arriving?"

"Yes. I just got here."

"This is my son Skeebo. He is actually a member of your Love Team, as I assume that is where you are headed."

"Skeebo, this is Dittims," Lakota introduced, "who belonged to Mary's mom, Christy, who is your caretaker. We all lived together in Alabama and in Iowa."

"Oh, that's neat," said Skeebo. "We will have to catch up with you soon and share stories. We are currently working on finishing a project together over in District 62. Since we are huskies and known as pullers of sleds, we help with moving supplies from project to project."

"Sounds like you need a horse to haul stuff around," teased Junior.

"Oh, they do for the bigger stuff," said Lakota, "but this is the last little bit, and we can easily handle it. Come over to Sector 80, Ninth Street when you get a chance. We are getting our house ready for Mary, my caretaker. You, remember Lucy? She is there working on the music library. You know how Mary loves her music."

"Yes, I do," said Dittims. "She loved singing in choirs as well as with the radio in the car. I remember her singing in the car on one of our trips."

"Lots of fun memories for family review time," said Lakota.

"And I will get over for family review time soon," said Skeebo, "once we get this delivery made and organized."

"Looking forward to it," said Dittims, wondering what family review time was as he turned and continued his journey.

When he saw the marker for District 51, he was amazed at the feeling pulling him inside. Once he turned in, he noticed that the street numbers were similar to the district numbers starting at number 1 as well. But when he turned down street number 9, the numbering similarities stopped. Some of sidewalks had a plate with a number system similar to what Sasha had told him to look for, and some had a pure white stone that was engraved with letters in a language that he could not read.

All of the homes were perfectly manicured with many colorful flowers beds scattered about the lawn or along the fronts and sides of each home. Some homes had people working in various areas of the yard or just sitting and enjoying being outside. There were even homes where Dittims saw other dogs or cats lying in the fresh air, rest-

OUR HOME OF LOVE

ing and watching him as he walked down the street. Some homes had hedge borders that were covered with tiny white bell-shaped flowers, and some had bushes that had been formed into shapes of animals or regal shapes as desired by each individual owner. Birds were singing in the trees, and butterflies were bouncing from blossom to blossom. Even the occasional hummingbird flew across his path heading to the next flower but went unnoticed as he held a steady pace going down the walkway toward his given direction.

At one point, the path curved sharply to the left, and the assigned home came into view. There was a small pond in the front with a small gentle fountain splashing in its center. There were several benches scattered around it, each with a different-color cushion. The house was small but bright with many windows to let in the natural light and its warmth. A box was beneath each window brimming with many bright-colored zinnias. The grounds surrounding the home had several raised beds filled with various types of flowers of different heights and colors. There was a winding sidewalk that curved toward the front door, and what appeared to be a small welcoming committee was resting there ready to greet him.

"Hello, I am looking for 904-TC4," he said as he approached the group.

A gentle but strong-looking German shorthaired pointer with a large spot over one ear nodded his head in assurance.

"This is it. We have been waiting on you and have heard much about you. Welcome aboard. My name is Spot Jr. III, but they call me Spot for short. I am the initial greeter for this house, your final home."

"Oh, I wonder if you are the Spot that I was named after. I guess you already know my full name is Spot Junior, but my family called me Dittims."

Chuckles and happy tail thumps on the decking were heard from the greeting members.

"Yes, we know," said Spot. "Your cutesy nickname compared to your giant size makes us chuckle, but we understand the love and character of Christy. We all have been loved by her at some point in her life. That being said, let me introduce you to the few that are here, and then I will give you a tour of the grounds before meeting the rest of the members. This small fry here is Nellie. She is the mother of our smallest member here, Sandra."

"Wow," said Dittims, "you gals look almost identical and so tiny. I will be extra careful not to step on you, guys. I had such disabilities before, but now it's amazing how wonderful things are for me. I can fully see and hear, so I should be able to maneuver my giant body more easily and avoid the mishaps like I have had before."

"We are small," piped up Sandra, "but quick on our feet, and that helps to not get stepped on by those bigger than us."

"This last lady is Gypsy," continued Spot. "She is one of our quieter members."

Gypsy tilted her head shyly, and with a happy tail thump on the deck, she explained, "I was just a mutt that was thrown away by my original caretaker but was lovingly taken in by Christy's family and of course fully loved by Christy. I was named by her father for my pronounced black skin around my eyes and lips against my tan color. He thought I looked like I was wearing makeup."

"It's nice to meet all of you. I am so very happy to be here," said Dittims.

"We always start off with a small group for introduction and tour of the grounds to help newcomers get acclimated and comfortable with their surroundings. So shall we begin?" asked Spot.

"I am going to bow out of the tour, Spot," said Gypsy, "as I want to help fix the flowers on the right side of the house that Trip is trying to work in. He is trying real hard but may be too small to do it correctly, causing the flowers to grow crooked."

Chuckles rumbled through the group as everyone knew Trip's hyper energy could sometimes be a hindrance when it came to small area gardening even though his heart was in full gear with what he was trying to do.

"Trip, is also my son," explained Nellie while shaking her head looking down at her feet before tilting her head back to meet Junior's eyes. "He takes more after his father's side though being black with a tan muzzle plus having that excess amount of energy."

OUR HOME OF LOVE

The group of four walked down to the pond, and each took a quick drink as they watched the small fish darting in and out under the lily pads.

"This water is cold like a mountain stream," commented Dittims after enjoying a good long drink.

"Remember the falls you saw when you crossed over the bridge coming here?" asked Spot.

"Yes, they are quite beautiful. The mist from it washed over me and made me feel renewed somehow."

"Yes, those are Welcome Falls. They represent the Master to mankind, well, all of creation really. Water is a life-giving resource. In Ezekiel 47:9, the prophet compares a river flow to that of the Master's love: 'Wherever the river flows, every living thing that moves will thrive.' It's a living entity. The Master himself spoke of living water while he was on earth. Several times, he spoke saying if anyone was thirsty to come to him to receive this living water. Those who receive this living water can then pass it on to others. It creates a cycle of love and peace. The water coming through the heart at Welcome Plateau is a show of how much he cares and gives freely of his love for everything, an outward gift of life that flows to every living being. And the water source originates in the big city where it flows down the middle of the main thoroughfare, creating a wonderful river that goes throughout all of the land. Wherever there is water, whether it is a river or creek, a large lake, or the small quiet ponds like this one, the water all starts from that same source."

"When I first got here, I remember seeing that river coming out of the city as I was on the bridge. It was hard to judge the distance from the bridge, so is the city far? Are we allowed to go there sometime?" asked Dittims.

"There will be plenty of time for that," explained Spot. "First, we need to you get fully acclimated with us and the basics of what we do. There is a sing off coming soon, and we all love to go to those. That would be a good first visit to the city. All of heaven will be singing in one accord. It's inspiring."

"Dittims, do you understand why we are all in this area and located at this final home?" asked Nellie.

"Well, I guess it was because that is where the Master has sent us?" said Dittims.

"That's true," said Spot, "but there is a purpose behind it. You will learn there is generally a purpose behind everything we do here. At this house, we are waiting on the arrival of your caretaker, Christy. This is her final home, and we were all loved by her at some point of her life and therefore are all members of her Love Team."

"Oh, now what Sasha said about Love Teams makes more sense," said Dittims. "I knew we were originally created as helpers like all animals but did not realize we would all get reunited one day with her in her final home."

"You see, Dittims," commented Nellie, "we as animals are kind of continuing on as we were originally created, as helpers for mankind. We were given distinct abilities to be able to feel things from the Master of knowing who we are and who he is. Plus, we have the ability to feel which people are tuned into him and which are not. It helps us be better helpers for our good caretakers and helps protect us sometimes from the poor caretakers."

"Even in the wild," said Spot, "the animals could feel the difference after the fall, but they were too scared of what was happening to trust man again."

"I wonder why mankind was not given these abilities," said Dittims as he watched a small turtle climb on top of a lily pad.

"They were originally," Nellie further explained, "but trickery and sin entered at the fall and the whole order of life and survival got changed."

"Now, man listens more to the world and what it says," commented Spot, "than listening to his inner heart and what the Master can show him. That's why there is so much sadness and grief with man. They have forgotten their first love, his love. It affects all of creation. But for us four here and the rest of our group, we were some of the fortunate ones. We had a good person taking care of us that was also close to the Master. Some of the gifts he gave her she shares with others now. Then once she gets here, she will use them even more."

"You will notice during our tour today," added Sandra, "as well as in future walks, that a lot of the things you will see on the grounds of this home are interests or favorite things of Christy's. Let's start with this small pond and fountain. She loves the light splashing sound it makes. It is peaceful to sit here with the nice breeze that usually flows through here and makes this area a wonderful place to relax and have quiet time. The benches are cushioned for us to sit on, or we can enjoy the grass. It is softer than any that I have laid on before. We usually come down here in groups because there is plenty of room for all of us."

"What are the other homes that I noticed as I walked to get here?" asked Dittims.

"Those are homes for other people who also loved and followed the Master," said Sandra. "Some people have already arrived, and some homes are still waiting like us. And not all homes are filled with the love of pets. The love and heart of the home comes from the one who will live here. That love could be from plants to children or whatever the love interest represents."

Spot turned the group toward the house to continue the tour as he was speaking. "Let us start moving toward the back of the house, shall we? This side of the home"—he nodded to his left—"is used for perennial flowers. Since we don't worry about seasons here, some flowers can bloom constantly, but we keep them separated just for clarification purposes as the majority of the perennial flowers planted here are ones Christy especially likes that can also be cut and taken into the house for enjoyment."

"Spot," called out a concerned voice as a long-haired mixed black lab came from around the front of the home. "Excuse me for interrupting. Hi, my name is Blacky," she said as she rushed up to the group. "Nice to meet you, but we have a situation on the annual side that needs your direction. Gypsy sent me as Ruth could not be disturbed."

"Trip," moaned Nellie and Sandra simultaneously as they lowered their heads knowing it was probably a bigger mess than what Gypsy has first thought before leaving the tour.

They all headed over to the annual side of the home to find over half of one bed totally dug up with flowers scatter in different piles by color and Trip's head covered in dirt.

"Trip," asked Spot in his gentle authoritative way, "what are you doing?"

"I am helping. Well, just trying to help get all the colors in order, and then we can…"

"Trip"—his mother spoke firmly but gently—"this isn't your person's final home. You can help if asked, but you don't have Christy's knowledge of what is favored."

Trip hung his head. "But I remember how nice Christy was, and I like to dig in the dirt, and my caretaker is not interested in gardens like Christy, and I wanted to help. And this bed had colors scattered everywhere."

"Is there a problem here?" asked one of the chefs as he came out to pick some tomatoes from the small garden.

"No, we just have a minor misunderstanding," assured Gypsy. "If you would please get in touch with one of the available gardeners, we might need a little help in getting this back into order."

"Sure thing," he agreed. "I will get that taken care of as soon as I take these tomatoes to the kitchen."

"Thank you," said Gypsy as he headed back inside.

"Have you tried to help down at the community garden?" asked Spot.

"Yea," said Trip with head hung low, "I don't think they like my digging either. They say that I go too fast and get things out of order."

"It's not that they don't like your digging or your speed Trip," explained Spot. "We all have gifts and talents given for specific purposes. Maybe yours is just not for small gardens. You need to find a place to satisfy your gift to dig, combined with the help it provides. Maybe it is not an actual garden you need to dig in but find some other use for digging. Have you been over to see Farmer Jones? He even has a construction project going on that you might be able to help with."

"No, I haven't, didn't really think about it. Do you think he will let me dig?" said Trip in excited rapid-fire questions, not really waiting on a response. "You know I really love to dig," he said; then he surveyed the mess he had made. "Sorry," he said softly and slowly. "Do you want me to stay and help fix this?"

OUR HOME OF LOVE

"No," said Gypsy quickly. "We have got this. You go see if you can find an avenue for your energy."

"Okay," said Trip, and he turned and raced off toward the farming community.

"Well," said Nellie, "he does have a good heart."

They all chuckled. "Gypsy, have you really got this?" Spot asked.

"I can help," offered Blacky.

"Sure, we have this, and maybe we will be done when you get back around to this side," confirmed Gypsy.

"Okay, then, let us resume our tour."

Chapter 3

*Love for all living creatures is the
most noble attribute of man.*
—Charles Darwin

As they came back around to the perennial side where they had started earlier, they were met by a tall regal-looking collie with long flowing light-colored hair heading their way.

"Hello, my name is Rusty. I heard you were coming and wanted to introduce myself."

"Hi, they call me Dittims."

After chuckling at the cutesy name, Rusty apologized, "Don't mean to laugh, but you are an awfully big guy for a cute little name like that."

"Yea, my real name is Spot Junior, but because of my disabilities at the time, my caretaker's daughter nicknamed me Dittims, and it kind of stuck."

"Yea, I knew Christy when she was a teenager. She was a real special character. I bet her daughter has some of the same quirkiness. Spot, are you going to have the family review talk later? I would like to join if I could. I have not participated in one in a while."

"Sure," said Spot, "we would love to have you join. Give us some time to tour the grounds."

"Okay, see you shortly." Rusty nodded as he headed out toward the road.

Continuing on, Spot began speaking again about the perennial gardens as they moved down that side of the yard.

"You will notice most of the flower beds are raised and not necessarily square in shape. They were created this way for a couple of reasons. Being raised makes it easier for people to work in them, but their shape is mostly due to Christy's personality. Christy is one of the artsy types and likes interesting shapes and colors. For instance, this garden over here"—he motioned as they walked up to a tiered garden—"while it is square, it has multiple levels with plants that help show off each different level. On the very top, you have your taller flowers like delphiniums, larkspurs, and gladiolus with a colorful mix of lilies on the next level. The next level down has various types of daisies and chrysanthemums with low-growing clump flowers on the lower level. This particular bed has a lattice backdrop where confederate jasmine grows, emitting its wonderful fragrance into the air. That is a particular favorite of Christy's. It is delightful, isn't it?" said Spot, fully inhaling the fragrance.

Dittims nodded as he also took in a refreshing breath.

"Is working in the garden a favorite activity that Christy does? I did not see much of that while I was with her."

"I think that while you were there, it was a time when work outside of the home was consuming a large portion of the day. But from what I hear, there were other outlets for her artistry, relaxing or getting away from the stress of any given day."

"Yes." Dittims nodded. "And some of it was quite comical."

"Well, I look forward to your stories during family review time."

"I keep hearing about family review time but don't understand what that is."

"Sorry," explained Spot. "We get so used to the terms we use that we sometimes forget newcomers may not understand what we are talking about. Family review is where all members of the love team get together, introduce themselves, and tell stories that occurred during their time with their caretaker. It is great fun, sometimes a little shocking but always amazing. Sometimes nonmembers, like

Rusty, want to come listen because of connections they may have had with a certain caretaker."

"Sounds intense," said Dittims.

"It's not, but there is so much new stuff being thrown at you right at first. We choose to slow it down with you meeting just a few members and exploring the grounds so you can get a good bearing on where you are. Then we will drown you," teased Spot as he bumped Dittims on the hip.

"Thank a lot." Dittims chuckled.

"It's all good, I promise. As we move more to the back of the house, you will begin to smell the different fragrant sections, with gardenias, roses, and various bushes that attract butterflies and hummingbirds." All members stopped to enjoy the various fragrances floating through the air.

"Around the gazebo, we have these low shrubs, some that flower and some with variegated leaf colors. Christy enjoys watching nature in all of its forms and is interested in the birds that flower gardens attract, especially the hummers. And the sweet flower smells have always been a top list item for her."

"I remember when she was young," commented Sandra, "that night blooming flowers whose fragrances would fill the air when the night air was still was always a favorite."

"The gazebo, you will notice," continued Spot, "is adjacent on one side to a long stretch arbor which is one of the entrances to the large garden maze. We all like to roam through the maze because it reminds us of the stories we hear describing the beauty of Eden. All homes have an entrance to the maze in similar fashion. The maze is filled with many types of vegetation beginning with low hedges on the front, large shade trees in the center, and more flower varieties throughout than you can count. Where mazes were at one time thought to be a game area for lost and found, this maze allows you to enjoy the abundant plant life around you. It helps you relax and feel the Master's presence. You may see him periodically as he comes and roams through different sections of it himself. He has always been partial to gardens."

OUR HOME OF LOVE

"You mean we get to walk in the garden with the Master," asked Dittims, "just like in Eden?"

"Just like in Eden," assured Nellie. "You remember how before we got here, we could speak with him through our hearts and prayers? So now we still get to do that, but this is his home, so we have times when he will meet with us."

"Can we relax a bit on the gazebo so I can process what I have heard so far and also view all that is here?" Dittims asked.

"Sure, from the gazebo, you can see the side of the house we just came from. And from here, you can smell the various fragrances that run all through the grounds. The very back of the land behind the maze is where the orchards and main gardens are planted, so we have fresh fruit or vegetables at any time."

"What type of vegetables?" Dittims asked, "I am partial to fresh broccoli and string beans."

The girls chuckled. "Yes, there is even a small vegetable garden near the house that has some of Christy's favorites that you will see when you resume your walk, and there are plenty of both of those there."

"This is nice," Spot remarked as he stretched out on a bench. "They just added these cushions to these benches, but I guess they are still a little short for you."

"Oh, they are just fine. I can sit on the bench 'like a peoples' as Christy used to tease. It takes the weight off my hips and allows me to rest while still keeping my front feet on the deck floor, ready to move. This is really a restful place."

"Yes, it is," agreed Spot quietly. "It is our own little piece of heaven."

"So you seem to be the lead, but you don't always refer to Christy as your caretaker as the girls do. Are you not a member of this house?" asked Dittims.

"No, not fully, I am what we call a part-timer. My caretaker is already here, and I stay with him mostly. But as you will learn, we all help out where we are needed. My caretaker was Christy's father, but I was the first love member on the scene that Christy remembers. Therefore, I come here and welcome newcomers and introduce them to the other members that are here to make this home ready for her arrival. I usually speak first at family review time to give a lot of the family dynamics needed to help the newcomers understand the whole picture."

"Do we know when Christy's arrival will be?"

"No," replied Spot. "That is up to the Master's timing, but we will be ready whenever that will be."

"Will I be the last Love Team member to arrive before Christy?"

"No. Actually, you have a replacement. Her name is Mimi." Spot grinned, shaking his head. "And in Christy's own words, 'She be crazy.' Arrival timing for all things is up to the Master and of course up to the individual for not getting into something they should not get into. There are a couple of our members that arrived earlier than they should have due to carelessness on their part. But you will learn that the Master always has a plan for any given situation depending on how the person or animal reacts."

"If we are here waiting on Christy, then what is our purpose here?" asked Dittims, looking around at his surroundings. "Everything looks ready to me."

"Well, it is, and it isn't. We are still fine-tuning our thoughts and actions to prepare for God's ultimate plan. Deuteronomy tells us when the words of God were handed to the people, he told them to love the Lord and to walk in his ways. We, man and beast, are still learning how to perfect that here. Each of us has a purpose to fulfill for the last days."

"Like what?" asked Dittims

"Before coming here, many people had jobs or strong interests that they enjoyed, and those interests have carried over to here. Like people who love to garden are gardeners at their own homes. Plus, they may help out at other homes of people that are not here. Some even help those that are here who don't care much for gardening. Or like the cooks that are currently in this kitchen, they are here helping us until Christy's arrival. We have the ability now for man and beast to work hand in hand as it was first intended. Plus, we all enjoy each other's company. And there are many other projects mankind does that we get to help with."

OUR HOME OF LOVE

After pondering his thoughts for a while, Dittims asked a question he had been wondering since he got there. "Why do we call him Master and people call him Lord? He really is Lord of all."

"True, mostly it is just semantics. He is our ultimate Master, and we were created for a specific purpose of helper where man was created in his image. Man has been given different types of gifts that are needed to help promote his kingdom. When the initial order was changed at the fall and the loss of Eden, the remainder of creation also lost their ability to work together for the good of the kingdom. Even in the animal world, we had to learn to fight to survive, which created a lot of anger, frustration, and lack of trust in everything."

"Understanding that makes the story of Noah and the animals even more interesting," said Dittims. "Think about it, you have confused and scared animals to once again have to trust man for survival."

"It shows us," said Spot, "just how much God loves all of his creation by sparing both man and beast and telling them to again repopulate the earth."

After a short rest, the girls made their leave to go take care of things they needed to tend to and left the two guys to converse on their own.

"You know," said Dittims, "I don't know a lot of what is in God's Word, but what I do know shows his continual love and guidance for most any situation you may find yourself in. And that is only because I heard Christy's reading. Think about other pets or even the wild animals that never got the privilege of that."

"God always has a way of showing himself to anyone or any living being if they will just seek him out," reminded Spot. "Just think about the beauty of the stars at night, or even the gracefulness of the tiniest flower."

"That is true. He is the creator of everything."

Chapter 4

> I have left naming you until the last.
> I have turned my name around and
> will call you dog, my friend.

Dittims stretched and said, "There sure is a lot to think about and, I guess, for me to learn. Let's continue our tour, shall we?"

"Sure. Let's head toward your left. That side of the house has the small garden."

"You will notice," continued Spot, "the abundance of shade trees on the property toward the back of the house with multiple shade-loving flowers growing around them. Most have a light fragrance, but those there under the windows at the back of the house are exceptionally nice. When those windows are open, their smell seeps all through the house. Some late afternoons, we will open those, so the house is filled with wondrous smells to sleep by."

As they came around the corner from the back to the side of the house, the small vegetable garden the girls were referring to came into view.

"There is an abundance of green beans, lima beans, carrots, broccoli, cauliflower, yellow squash, red potatoes, tomatoes, and baby watermelons. Then these three trees are fruits trees with one peach, one orange, and one apple. These vegetables and fruits are some of Christy's favorites and provide easy access without having to go out to the main orchard or vegetable garden. That is where all of creation can enjoy any kind of vegetable or fruit you can think of. Some I have not even tried yet, and I have been here a good while."

"Oh, I see Gypsy and Blacky are gone, so they must have finished Trip's endeavors," commented Dittims.

"Yes, let's go see how they fared."

The flowers had been replanted back into an acceptable state with height being the factor and the color variety being mixed to add interest to the bed. One section was left empty with a large indention showing that something still needed to be added or maybe plants had been too damaged to replant.

"Looks like one of the gardeners may have a little extra work to do to get the bed back into a pristine state. Let's go see if we can find Gypsy."

As they went around to the front, Dittims took in the beauty around him. The morning was bright and clear with the air being crisp without being too cool yet was also warm. It was like a spring and a summer day meeting at the same time. Down by the pond, Dittims saw Gypsy, Nellie, and Sandra talking to others; so he and Spot headed down in that direction.

"Hello, boys, how was the tour?" asked Gypsy as they came up to the group.

"Relaxing and wonderful." Dittims sighed gently.

"I see there is still work to be done in the flower bed?" inquired Spot.

"Oh, yes. First, let me introduce Dittims to everyone. Dittims is the newest member of our home. Dittims, this is Brownie to my left and Tip to my right."

"Nice to meet you," said Dittims.

"Tip was telling me," said Gypsy, "they just replanted one of their flower beds over at Nann Manor and have bird's nest evergreens left over. They would go perfect there."

"That's a good idea. Has a gardener been assigned to complete the work?"

"I am not sure," explained Gypsy, "as Ruth will need to finalize all of that."

"Are we about ready for the family review time?" asked Gypsy. "Brownie, your stories are welcome since you were part of the extended family, and, Tip, you knew Christy when she was young, that is if either of you have time."

"We would love to, but we have prior commitments. We promise to catch up at a later date, though."

"That would be good. See you when there is more time."

As the two friends turned to leave, Gypsy explained that Brownie had belonged to Christy's grandmother and that Tip had belonged to a neighbor across the street when Christy was young.

The group turned to head up to the house, only to pause momentarily at the sound of small pounding footsteps and a constant "Spot… Spot… Spot" that could be heard echoing down the hill. Trip was in full run with legs, tongue, and slobber flying in all directions. Mother and sister moaned quietly knowing this could be bad.

"Y'all won't believe what just happened. I am so excited. I can't believe it myself. It's so very exciting. I…"

"*Trip*," exclaimed Sandra, "relax."

"Okay. Okay, sorry. I just get excited sometimes," he explained as he came to a skidding stop.

"We know," soothed Nellie as the others chuckled. "Now what is so exciting?"

"Well, you know I went to see Bill Jones. His wife, Sarah, likes daisies, but with the farm that needs to run and the new construction project, she has not had the time to plant. So she said I could do it. She will show me the area she wants planted and get me the daisies, and I can do whatever I want…within reason of course. It's all so exciting," he exclaimed as he turned around in circles.

"Trip, that's great news," warned his mother, "*but* you must remember to remain calm and not get so excited that you don't do the job as intended."

"I'll be calm… I'll be calm." And with that comment, he tore off toward his final home.

OUR HOME OF LOVE

"Oh," moaned Nellie, "he is so his father's son, but he is learning the Master's ways." They all chuckled as they moved up the sidewalk toward the front door. As they hit the front doormat, the door automatically opened.

"That makes it easy to enter," said Dittims.

"Well, it's not like we have hands to turn a doorknob." Spot chuckled. "Although, I have known dogs and horses that could maneuver certain types of handles to gain entrance or exit as needed."

"Well, in our case," said Sandra, looking at her mom, "we would never be able to reach the doorknob."

Dittims chuckled. "That is for sure."

Inside, Dittims was surprised to feel the comfort he felt as he walked into the main hallway, like coming home after being away for a while. The entryway was wide with doors on both sides going down the hallway. The first room on the left side of the hall had plenty of room with several oversized padded sofas and a large desk near the far windows. As Dittims poked his head into the room, he noticed the wall to the right of the doorway and its adjacent wall were lined with books from the floor to ceiling. Then a ladder on a rail was connected to both walls, allowing a reader the ability to reach any book. The opposite end of the room from the books was the front windows for that side of the home. The windows started about a foot off the floor, making it easy to see the beauty of the grounds when inside. The room was comfortable in temperature, but more so, it had a calm peaceful feel to it.

Voices from a room further down the hall summoned them to come there. So they came out of the library and moved toward the voices. Dittims noticed before they headed down the hall that the door opposite the library on the right side of the hall was closed, but it had a bright light coming from under the door.

When they entered the room down the hall where everyone was talking, Dittims saw that it was an elongated room with no furniture. The floor was covered in soft plush carpet where the library had been a smooth polished wooden floor like the hallway. All around the room were large over stuffed cushions, and on each cushion sat a different member of this Love Team. Each cushion was made for the size and shape of the team member.

As they both entered the room, Spot motioned toward the fireplace to two very large members who occupied their equally large cushions. "I believe you know each other," he said to Dittims.

"Azer," yelled Dittims as he ran and gave Azer, his brother, a firm neck hug. "Gosh, you look great." He turned and noticed another likeness and made a guess. "I bet you are Gracie."

Gracie cocked her head to the side in approval and nodded. "You are very astute. Yes, I am Gracie, the first member of the giants for our Christy."

"I assume that other large cushion belongs to you, Dittims," said Spot, chuckling, "amongst your equally sized family members. Those oversized cushions would swallow most us completely. But I am sure some of us who would love to periodically stretch out and wallow fully on it. So you may have to run someone off once in a while."

As Spot looked around the room, he saw the center cushion by the window was empty. This was a special meeting, and everyone was aware that they were to be present, especially Ruth, the canine lead.

"Where's Ruth?"

"With the Master," explained a sleek black short-haired member of the team.

"Concerns?" he asked cautiously.

"Nope, just observing the replacement," she explained with a grin.

"Well, that replacement has the same energy level you did, Munchkin," Spot teased, nodding toward the sleek member.

"Yes, I know. But as much as it pains me to admit it, she is a lot smarter than I was. No comments needed from the rest of you, thank you very much," she said as she looked around the room. Then the room burst into loving laughter, including Munchkin's own giggles.

"Any idea how long she will be?" Spot prompted.

"Probably not too long," said a voice from behind Spot as Rusty entered the room. "I heard them finishing up as I came in the front door."

OUR HOME OF LOVE

The closed door, thought Dittims as he pondered the situation.

"Well then, Rusty, pull down an extra cushion, and get comfortable. Dittims, you take the empty cushion by Azer. From that position, you will be able to see everyone clearly as they tell their story. Once this family review is done, positions of cushion on the floor really don't mean anything."

"Except," reminded Sam.

"Yes, I understand how y'all do things here, but that is not a requirement," he remarked.

"We do it out of respect, Spot, not requirement," said Nellie.

"Does she understand that?" asked Spot.

"Yes," explained Gypsy. "While she just feels it is 'most unnecessary' as she would say, she has conceded to accept it. She knows we do it out of love and respect not only for her but also for the relationship she had with Christy and all that she does for us here."

"An honorable deed indeed," agreed Spot, quietly nodding his head.

"Excuse me," queried Dittims. "Can you fill me in so that I am aware of what we are talking about? I remember Ruth as she was there when I first got there, but I am lost in what y'all are referring to."

"Sorry, didn't mean to sound so secretive," said Gypsy. "Ruth, Baby Ruth or Miss Ruth, depending on who you are talking to at the time, is the favorite member of all of us. While we all had a special allotment of shared time with Christy, Ruth got the closest with her and was the most in tuned with her. She was there at an especially hard time of Christy's life. Therefore, we honor Ruth by letting her have the pick of spots depending on the day. She used to refuse us for it, but she now understands that it is an honor to her from us and to please not refuse our gift."

"Wow," said Dittims. "I had forgotten a lot about her before coming here. She was there when I first arrived. I was so young, and while Christy was not aware of my special needs, Ruth was and was very nurturing to me. I was so handicapped with my deafness and blindness in one eye that I always wondered if there may have been important things I missed because of those issues."

"No," assured Spot, "did you feel Christy's love?"

"Every day." He nodded.

"Then there you go, the rest is just gravy."

A quiet hush fell over the room as the Master and Ruth entered the room. The Master looked each one in the eye with more love than you could imagine, and with a gentle nod, he said his good-byes and left the room. Ruth came full into the room and sat on her cushion. Her leadership role of the home is not only because of her calm and mothering nature but also due to her keen understanding of his ways.

"So we have a new member today," she said gently. "Welcome, Dittims, it's good to see you again. Have you met everyone?"

"Not formally, no."

"Okay, let's do that first. Of course you have met Spot and a few of the girls, but let's go around the room in case someone has to leave, and we will introduce new friends as they arrive. Starting from my right is Gypsy, whom you met earlier. Then to my left is one you should remember, Munchkin, and by her are Nellie and her daughter Sandra. By the fireplace are faces you are familiar with, your brother Azer, and sister Gracie. Coming on around past you is Zero, then Sam, short for Samantha, and lastly Rusty is a family friend.

"Today, we will start family review time with a few stories from each member, and then we will hear a few of your stories. The length of time it takes for family review may take a while. So we brake periodically for walks, food, events, and so on. Different members and nonmembers will drop in and out as we go, but we have lots of time to get you acclimated. During each member's story time, remember no storyteller is more important than the next. We are all very important members of this particular Love team. We were introduced into Christy's life at a time when the Master sent us to build a special relationship during a particular time and situation of Christy's life—no time more important that the rest, just different."

"Some members of Love families," explained Spot, "are the means by which the Master helps the different caretakers cope with particular or difficult circumstances of life. Some member's stays are long, some are short, and some quick visits may not really be team members but one-time intervention helpers."

"So," said Ruth as she looked over the room, "shall we do this chronologically? That makes the most sense to me."

With nods around the room, the format was set. The stories would begin with Spot since he was the first love member on the scene when Christy was very young.

Chapter 5

> All animals should be treated as the wonderful creations from God that they are.

Spot pulled his cushion more to the center of the room for all to see him clearly.

"Since I am first to begin, I will explain for Dittims's sake that not all of us were in full-time partnership with Christy. Rusty, for instance, as mentioned earlier, is not even a real member of this Love Team, but because he had such a strong bond with your caretaker when she was a teenager, he has asked to be here tonight. Gypsy, as you also learned, was not an original team member but was adopted in when Christy was an early teenager. And, of course, Munchkin, the sassy high-energy one of the group, originally belonged to one of the Christy's sons, but sometimes people get into situations where they can not properly take care of us. I explain this so that you can see that the makeup of the Love Teams doesn't necessarily reflect ownership of man to dog as much as they reflect love, so that is why we sometimes have an overlap of members."

"Fortunately for all of us here," said Ruth, "Christy had a strong love for all of us. Therefore, we wound up as members in this Love Team. And there are others who were also part-timers in the family that will drop in periodically with interesting tales about their experiences during their time with Christy."

"I also want you to know things are not as rigidly structured as it may seem with all of us gathered here in this one room. As Ruth explained, we will take breaks periodically and experience more of the grounds, and then of course, there is always time for food and fun activities. The main goal and purpose for family review is for you to get to know us and to understand what it was like for our particular time with Christy. And of course, we can't wait to hear your stories. But for starters, let me give you a visual of the original home and grounds that Christy grew up in."

Spot nestled comfortably on his cushion and leaned back in remembrance.

"The original homestead was located in South Georgia just north of the Florida line in a small but growing town. The homestead originally was open farm land that had been subdivided for homes and was located just north of the growing business district.

"Christy's father and his oldest brother both built their homes on large lots next to each other on the same side of the street. The street and driveways at that time were still dirt, and the remaining land not yet purchased had very few trees, being mostly open sage grass fields.

"The two brothers saw the vision of what the area could be as the town was destined to grow out in their direction, and they planted young southern magnolia trees on both sides of the dirt lane in front of their two houses. When they got big, their beautiful large white and fragrant blossoms in the spring were delightful. They also planted pecan trees in various spots on the property, so when grown, they would add much-needed shade during the hot summer months. The front of the house was planted with lots of young pine trees to go with the abundant azalea bushes that banked the front of the house. When these trees got big, they would also provide shade and would almost sing as they gently swayed in the breeze. I remember lying under them listening as the breeze moved to wherever it was going."

Spot paused for a moment as he remembered back to those magical times.

"On the east side of the home was a fenced-in pasture for CJ's horse, Miss Priss, a graceful paint. The home originally was a rectangle in shape, but as the family grew, an addition had been added off the back center of the home, giving it a *T* shape. The home was white with green shutters and two white dormers for the second floor. It really was a wonderful place to call home, especially once the trees gained enough size to add shade and character.

"Now," he stated as he sat more upright, "let's talk about how I came onto the scene and interacted with Christy. I was a young pup given to Christy's father because of his love for hunting birds. My father had been the German shorthaired pointer champion hunter for two years running. His caretaker needed some work done by Christy's father as he was a lawyer. Evidently, their conversation included the enjoyment of duck hunting, and I was given as a gift.

"Unfortunately"—he paused as soft giggles were heard around the room, for they had heard his story many times—"I took more after my mother than father. I remember thinking as a young pup, 'Really, you want me to get in the cold water to go fetch a *dead* bird in my mouth…? No, don't think so. Do y'all have any idea know cold it is out here? Give me the warm rug in front of the fireplace, and I will be just fine.'"

"And you still favor the fireplace." Sam chuckled as she teased Spot.

"As do you, my friend."

"Yea, but I am a basset. While my breed can be fine hunters, we would really rather lie down somewhere and sleep." Loving laughter filled the room.

"Well, I don't have a lot of stories to tell you about Christy as I was an older fellow when she came on the scene, but I do remember a few. First, let me describe this crazy sleeping contraption she had. While it was bed for small children, it was more like a screen box. Her room was lovingly called the Little Room but had originally been a dressing room before the addition was added.

"Since homes did not have air-conditioning during that time as windows were screened and left open for air flow on those hot summer evenings. Those pesky mosquitos could sneak through the tiniest screens or zip in when doors were opened. I remember snapping at them as they hovered in the doorway when I would ask to come in."

"The box bed you speak of, do you mean it was made out of cardboard?" asked Dittims.

"No," replied Spot, "it had wooden posts on the corners for support, but the sides were screen mesh like screen on a window, and it had a flip overtop that was also that same screen material."

"I guess to keep the little tyke safe from bugbites," pondered Dittims.

"Yes," replied Spot, "and evidently very effective until she was old enough to figure out how to open the top. Then they had to place her in a small junior-size bed to keep her from trying to climb out and falling."

"I do remember many times of her climbing all over me before finally snuggling down to sleep while I was on the rug in front of the TV. There never was a fear of any animals even from a young age with Christy. She always seemed to be in tuned with us and has kept that great love and respect for all animals. As all of you know, we can feel that love, anger, and even fear from people as they interact with us. As we have mentioned before, it is through these abilities given to us by the Master that help us detect who the good caretakers are versus the bad. Unfortunately, there are some not so good caretakers."

"Yes," commented Ruth, "there has always been a strong bond with Christy and all of the Master's creations. Wait." Ruth shuddered in remembrance. "I best clarify that. While there is a great respect for all creation, there are many things none of us, man or beast, want anything to do with." Soft chuckles and nods of affirmation went around the room.

"Got to close to that slithery creature on the walk in the woods, didn't you?" teased Gypsy.

"Yes," said Ruth, "and thanks to the quick hand of the Christy's son, he got us out of the way and killed that disgusting thing with a stick. I still shudder thinking about it."

"Life was full of interesting events living with Christy and her family," said Spot.

"Tell us about the story in the barn," asked Zero. "It is such a wonderful story of how we can all work together, man and beast, if we just will try.

"Okay, but this is a story that happened toward the middle of my time. Dittims, you will find that sometimes stories get told more out of similarity or love of the story than the actual time line of its occurrence. Remember the fenced-in area for Miss Priss? Well, inside that area, there was also a one stall barn, and next to that was the small shed where feed and supplies were kept. All of the children in the family had a love for all animals, but their mother had a great fear of Miss Priss. It was not that she did not care for the larger-sized animals, I think it was due more to fear and misunderstanding as she always had small pets like Nellie and then of course her love for bassets.

"Miss Priss was a gentle brown-and-white paint with a big heart, very much like her caregiver CJ. Once Christy was old enough to walk around good, she learned quick how to open the doors and sneak outside. By that time, the neighborhood had begun to grow, and some of the busier roads were no longer dirt. Quite a few more houses had been built on that street and nearby other growth including small businesses, a fire house, a plan for a new elementary school, and even plans for a larger hospital to be built in the area. So a small child out walking about alone could be a scary thing." Knowing nods went around the room.

"The family housekeeper, Katrina, was in the kitchen preparing the noonday meal, and she heard me barking just outside and scratching on the door. But when she came to the door, she saw me take off toward the barn and then noticed Miss Priss also acting all kinds of crazy in the back of her stall. She called for Christy's mom, and together, they went to see what the commotion was all about. I led the way showing them what the problem was. Young Christy had snuck outside without anyone realizing it to go see Miss Priss. She loved to walk under Miss Priss and scratch her belly."

"Now," said Spot, explaining further, "it was not really a far distance to the barn, but by the time everything that needed exploring was explored, Christy got tuckered out and decided to curl up in the doorway of the barn and take a nap. Miss Priss was not going to risk stepping over her to get out to the pasture, so she was a bit uneasy."

"I just love this story." Nellie sighed. "That happened shortly before I came on board."

"What happened then?" asked Dittims.

"Well, it actually was quite comical to watch. Christy's mom and Katrina both were terrified of Miss Priss and were in a real quandary worrying over the safety of the child. Her mom called her, but that didn't work, so she climbed through the fence into the pasture area and eased up to the side of the barn. She was able to reach around the corner of the barn door and grab Christy by the foot. She pulled her close and trotted back out the fenced area while Miss Priss gained access to the pasture area. Her mom took her back inside to continue her nap in safety. She didn't even wake up when being picked up with all that commotion."

"That story shows how we can to work together to help all of creation as the Master had first intended," commented Sandra. "And I think it's amusing that now man is discovering how different species of us do actually interact with each other as friends. People are so amazed by how much love we can show as well. I long for the day when we can get back to that everywhere, not just here."

"All in his timing," affirmed Zero, "all in his timing."

"How long were you there before coming here?" asked Dittims.

"For about four years after Christy came along then, Nellie came on the scene during my last year. Our stories will show you not only what we enjoyed while we were with Christy but also show you how times changed through the many generations represented in this room."

"Now," clarified Spot, "I think we need to go back to one of the earliest stories. It will give you some good indications of how Christy's personality developed as she grew."

Chapter 6

*The treatment of animals reflects
the character of your soul.*

As Spot adjusted his position, he leaned back on his cushion in thought. "I think the rocking chair story should be told. It was one of the first stories I remember and around the time when Christy was learning how to balance."

"It also shows," said Nellie, "her determination and the beginning of her athletic abilities."

"Let's first describe the interior layout of the house," said Spot. "When standing in the living room with the front door behind you, you were looking through a wide archway into the dining room. The kitchen was around the corner to the left from the dining room, and the children's bedrooms were to the right off the living room. There were two doors in the right back corner of the dining room with the one on the right going to the laundry room. The other doorway that went straight back was the addition part of the home. It had a master suite including a den, a bathroom, and a large bedroom for the mother and father. Off that bedroom was the garage."

"Sounds like a big house," said Dittims. "Did you have favorite place?"

OUR HOME OF LOVE

"Why, in front of the TV of course," stated Spot with a smirk. "Since they had closed up the fireplace in the living room, the old-style TVs of that time gave off warmth that felt good to my old bones. The TV was located on the left side of the arch at an angle so that anyone in the living room would be able to see it clearly."

"So on one side of the arch was the living room, and the other side was the dining room?" asked Dittims. "Really just one big room?"

"Yea, pretty much," said Nellie.

"One day," continued Spot, "as we were waiting on the noon-day meal, I noticed Christy was sitting in her little red rocker but was very intent on the TV. I thought it odd as that interest had never been there before, so I tried to see what could be so interesting about some guy doing exercises to show women how to slim down. Then I watched Christy get up and walked to the side of the TV, but she was looking above it. She went back to where she had been sitting and turned back to the TV and stared at it again. I got up to see what she was looking at and saw nothing. Then after a moment, I saw it. My old red ball that I had not played with in years was sitting on the top edge of the TV. I looked back at her to see if that was really what she was looking at, and that seemed to be the case. Then I saw her pull her chair to the side of the TV. I realized she was intent on reaching that ball. It was too high for me, or I would have tried for it. I knew this could be a problem, but her mom was in the back of the house folding clothes. When I went to go get her, she didn't realize why I was whining and told me to hush because I had just come in from outside. So I ran to Katrina in the kitchen, who was busy preparing the food. She didn't notice my panicked state until we all heard the screams from the living room. As everyone came running, we saw the small rocking chair was lying on its side, and Christy was sitting by it, crying with blood oozing from her mouth down her chin. The red ball had been reached but now had rolled on the floor under the dining table. Her mom picked her up to assess the damage while Katrina reached down with a tissue and picked up a small white object off the floor—Christy's tooth."

Several gasps were heard around the room.

"I don't think I have ever heard that story," claimed Rusty.

"Yea, mom and child both cried, and everyone came to a realization that this tyke was a climber and needed to be watched more carefully. The rocker was placed back upright and put in its regular place. Then I picked up the ball and put it in the rocker."

"What about the tooth?" asked Rusty.

"It was a baby tooth and, of course, no way to fix that issue but to wait on the permanent tooth to come in," offered Gypsy. "And that tooth took a long time coming in due to damage to the root. It was still out when I came along. Although it was rather comical sometimes when she was mad at someone. She would stick her tongue out sideways at them through the gap that was created."

"Well, I can see the comical side was there even at the beginning," said Dittims, chuckling at the vision in his head.

"There was help from her mother on that comical creative side as well involving tape and a pink bow. Let me tell this last story, and then the next person can have a go. Due to the fact that Christy had very little hair until she was three years of age, she was often mistaken for a little boy," explained Spot.

"The road on the other side of Miss Priss's pasture was still dirt but was also the back side of a small business strip that faced the next road over, which was becoming a new main street of growth going to the north side of the developing town. That dirt road extended on each end to two access roads that hit this new main road. One of the access roads was the road for the fire station and the new proposed school for that area. And the other end was the access street for the developing neighborhoods to have access to the new main road. The neighborhood access road had a new drug store on the corner that faced the new main road. And inside this drug store was a section where they served sandwiches and beverages for people stopping by to visit each other. There were not many restaurants at that time, and the drug stores were the front runners of the fast-food restaurants we are familiar with today. Once the fast-food chains started, the fountains, as they were called, went away, and those stores then became stores only for getting medication."

"Those store changed again in later years," commented Zero.

"That's true. Well, one day, Christy decided she would ride her new tricycle up to that drugstore and get an ice cream. She had been there with her mom and her grandmother, knew the way, so she made the decision to go by herself."

"Now," explained Spot, "let me clarify this story as I am telling it from me hearing it from the adult members of the family as they retold it. I was not present to tell what happened in the store. I had been left inside the home when Christy once again gained access to the outside without anyone knowing of her whereabouts. It was a Saturday afternoon, so traffic was less than normal. That dirt side road got very little traffic, but it was just one block away from a very busy road. The front of the store faced the busy road, but the entrance was located on the access road side. Evidently, there was a person leaving the store when Christy got there, which allowed her to slip into the building unnoticed at first. Once inside, she knew where the ice cream was located and headed in that direction. She managed to climb into one of the booth seats and sat down. Mr. Perry, the owner of the store, recognized Christy as he knew her mom but did not see her mom anywhere in the store. With Christy being dressed in overalls due to her rough and tumble nature and also having very little hair, Mr. Perry assumed she was a little boy and called her mom to let her know her son was in his store."

"Oh no," said Dittims.

"I remember him calling as I was on the floor watching Ben play with his blocks. 'Mr. Perry,' her mom explained, "I appreciate your call, but my son is right here. I think you may have the wrong family.' But as he described the child, her mom knew it was Christy and let him know she was on her way. From that day forward, she was no longer dressed in overalls, although it was probably the better type of clothing needed for this busy little person," said Nellie. "Her mom found some way to put a bow of some sort in what little hair she had even if it meant using tape to help distinguish that this little person was indeed a little girl."

Chuckles flitted around the room.

"That is such a cute story, but if something like that would have happen in later times, the child could have been hit by a car or worse," said Zero.

"True." Everyone nodded.

"You know," commented Sam, "I remember when that store was torn down and a hamburger shop was put up in its place. It created an entirely different traffic situation, and that's when that dirt road got paved. Cars would fly down that short back street coming to or going from the hamburger shop to bypass the main street traffic."

"They call it progress," said Rusty in quiet remembrance. "That road was on the front of my home, and I almost got hit once by some young teenager thinking he was cool by speeding down that street."

"Times really change from my era to yours Rusty," commented Spot, "and even more so now. Progress is a double-edged sword, slicing into the future with new technology but at the same time slicing off a lot of the morals and love that was so intended to remain important as deemed by the Master."

"Are you done for now, Spot?" asked Ruth. "We probably need a good stretch before we continue. Is everyone staying for the midday meal?"

"Good timing on my part," exclaimed Samson as he entered the room. "Hello, everyone."

"Hey, Samson," welcomed Ruth, "glad you could make it. Samson, this is Dittims, our newest member. Dittims, Samson was one of our short term members."

"Nice to meet you, Dittims. It is a wonderful day for a celebration of new arrivals," said Samson. "I can't stay long, but I wanted to come say hello, and food is always a bonus." He chuckled heartily.

"Shall we go out to the gazebo?" queried Ruth. "I will meet you out there after I go check to see how the meal is coming."

"Sure," said Spot.

"Samson, why were you a short time member?" asked Dittims as they walked through the yard toward the gazebo.

"I came along during Christy's adult years. I was the first dog she had gotten once all the kids were born. While Christy and the kids had a special love for all of us, her partner did not feel the same toward dogs, and she feared it was becoming too much of a strain on the family and me. She had heard of a program for specialty training of retrievers into search and rescue with the local law enforcement teams. She took me there, and they accepted me. We hugged and cried when we parted. It was a sad time for both of us, but I did enjoy my new caretaker and learned much from him, even had some significant rescues that I received credited for," he stated as they settled on the benches of the gazebo.

"That's amazing," said Dittims.

"All in the plan I am sure." Samson nodded. "So you are a big guy. What types of activities do you like doing?"

"Well, until coming here, I had minimal hearing and was fully blind in one eye, so about the only thing I did much outside of walking on the property with Christy was the cup toss."

"Cup toss?" commented several at once.

"Yea," said Dittims, chuckling. "It was great fun. You see," he paused as he remembered back. "Christy had great affection for this frozen cola-flavored treat that she would get at the gas station. When she finished the treat, there would always be a little left in the bottom of cup and she would give it to me. I would finish what was in the cup. Then I would have a great toy until I destroyed it from playing too hard with it. I would take it and toss it high into the air and try to catch it. Or I would throw it in the air and race around this large bush that was in the yard and swing by to pick it up as I raced by."

Giggles from the girls made the guys chuckle as well.

"It was a very simple life," he said, nodding his head.

"It sounds like you would be a good fit for our team," commented Spot as he got comfortable on the gazebo.

"Team for what?" asked Dittims.

"Well, actually there are several types. There is the tennis ball team, the foam ball team, which usually involves water, but I was thinking because of your size and possible running abilities you may be great for the Frisbee team. Do you know how high you can jump?" asked Spot.

"Not a clue."

"Let's not rush things, guys. Let Dittims get his bearings first," Ruth said in her gentle mothering way as she came onto the gazebo.

"We will," assured Zero. "We are just sizing him up for team capabilities."

"Oh, good grief," groaned Munchkin, "you guys never stop."

"No fun in that." Rusty chuckled. "Besides, there are really no winners in these games, as we have already won, but the picnic food and great company always makes a fabulous combination."

"That's true," piped up Sandra. "There are even games for us little girls, and I am especially fond of the chasing games through the maze."

"My favorite part is after the games are done and the eating is complete, we nestle with our caretakers for some quiet time," replied Rusty.

After a few minutes of quiet, Dittims asked, "But if our caretaker is not here yet, what do we do?"

In calming reassurance, Sandra explained, "There are many here that never had pets to love on, so we get to be with them. They are so glad that we are here with them, and there is always a lot of love to go around. The Master makes it all come together as it should."

"And some of us," teased Gracie, "don't do the games at all. We head straight for the loving."

Chuckles rolled around the gazebo in reflection of great times they had had during the many games, and even relaxing times they had been a part of.

"It amazes me that you big guys love to sit in laps like the little dogs," said Gypsy, "but the funniest part of it is while you may be sitting in a lap, your feet are on the ground."

"Perks for our size," teased Azer.

"Whoa," exclaimed Dittims as he ducked his head from a close buzzing sound that ripped near his head. "What was that?"

"That is a hummer," explained Gracie. "Our breed has to be careful where we sit so that our large size is not in the normal path of those creatures getting to their food. You see that large orange trumpet vine wrapped around the post behind you? That is where it was heading and those blooms are just about head high for you. I

OUR HOME OF LOVE

suggest you come over here to sit on this side away from the vines. Plus from this advantage, you can watch them. They really are amazing creatures."

"I am more partial to the gentle floating and fluttering of the butterflies," commented Dittims as he adjusted his location on the gazebo. "They move much slower."

"You will get used to it," assured Ruth as she grinned at his slight discomfort, which she found interesting from such a large creature.

"Well, shall we go to the next story while we are out here? Food will be served on the patio when it is ready. It is very comfortable here, and the breeze is nice," commented Ruth.

"That is a good idea," agreed Munchkin. "Do you have any more to talk about Spot, or are we moving on to Nellie?"

"No, I think I am done for now. More may come to mind at a later discussion. But I believe I have given a good base to start on, and, Nellie, you are the next in line."

Chapter 7

> Sometimes only a dog can fill the
> emptiness of your heart.

Nellie pulled a cushion more into the center of the gazebo for all to see her better.

"Hello everyone. While some of you are specific in your breed, I am just a basic run of the mill terrier mix."

"There is nothing basic about any of us," encouraged Ruth. "In reality, most of us are mixed, just different sizes."

"I know. It's just sometimes the stories or the adventures of others seem so much more exciting that some of what I did."

"I know how you feel," said Ruth, "but remember we all had a specific mission according to his plan. And you were with Christy when she was still very young."

"I know," said Nellie. "I came as a gift to the family from the grandfather's farm on the mom's side. There were six of us that were born in the back of one of the old tobacco barns on the west side of the property. The foreman of the farm found us and made sure we all got good homes."

"Was your mom his dog?" asked Rusty.

"Yes, and he knew puppies were coming, so he kept watching for us to be born. When I first got to Christy's family, Spot was still

OUR HOME OF LOVE

there but was getting on in years, and Christy, of course, was very young. But you know, even at that age, there was a special kindness that came from her that showed a special compassion she had toward animals that we could all feel."

"As my learning here increases," said Spot, "I am a firm believer this is a nurturing gift God gives man. Continue on with your story, Nellie."

"Okay," Nellie said with a slight giggle. "You all know my son Trip and how he loves to dig." Smiles and nods went around the room.

"But he just really wants to help," encouraged Zero. "He is still fine-tuning his talented purpose."

"Yes, he is, and in truth," Nellie continued, "he gets it honest. His father was a hyper guy, and I love to dig too, so he can't help himself. It is probably part of our terrier breed as well. Anyway, that is one of the things Christy and I loved to do together outside. Not planting anything, just digging holes and exploring the earth, like treasure hunting. We would find rocks of different colors and shapes that she would save and once we found an Indian arrow head."

Nellie was quiet for a moment thinking on which story to tell.

"I remember one beach trip in particular when the family went for vacation, and I got to go along. When we got to the beach, the older kids went straight for the water. Her mom took up a spot for reading under an umbrella, staying out of the sun, but Christy and I headed to the beach just above the water's edge with buckets and shovels in hand. I remember these neat little clam-type creatures of different colors that would bury themselves in the wet sand. We would dig them up just to watch them bury themselves again. They had so many color variations of yellow, purple, blue, and red. Some were solid in color, and some were stripped. Sometimes on the beach, you would find their shells empty, and when you opened the shell, it looked like tiny angel wings. It was a fun time."

"Those are coquina clams," chimed in Sam. "I remember when Christy was a teenager, she still liked to play with those things."

"Yes," continued Nellie. "We would spend hours doing that and building buckets of sand on top of each other making grand castles.

They would get decorated with the various shells and seaweed that were all over the beach. When the tide started coming in, we would watch as the waves would slowly dissolved our creation back into the ocean. We also liked taking walks along the beach with family members looking for shells that had been washed up from high tides. She had two separate boxes—one for larger shells, and one for little shells. When she would get home, she would take cigar boxes that she got from her father and would glue the shells she found to the top of them. Then she would give it to her mom or grandmother as a gift who thought they were wonderful. I wasn't so sure, but everyone was happy with their gift, so it was all worth it. Plus, I got some good lap time while she was gluing, sometimes with help from brother Ben. It was a great time."

Warm thoughts filled their minds as they all remembered similar situations, as lap time was always a special memory.

"Oh, looks like the food is being brought out," noted Gypsy as she looked toward the house to see large bowls being placed out around the patio. And I believe that fresh cut broccoli is a main item just for you, Dittims."

"Oh, broccoli is also one of my favorites, raw or cooked," commented Ruth. "I remember Christy preparing it for their meal but would also give me pieces of stems as she cut them up."

"Are all the vegetables raw? I think I smell butter and other deliciousness as well," commented Dittims as they left the gazebo and headed to the patio.

Scattered about the patio were multiple bowls of steaming vegetables, some mixed with various grains, some with butter, some plain, and some were raw vegetables. Then to the side were various bowls of chopped apples, plums, and watermelon. Everyone including those who had prepared the food gathered together with heads lowered in grateful thanks.

"Wow," commented Dittims, looking at all of the bowls, "this is a feast."

Muffled laughter from mouths full of food filled the air. "Wait until you see game day," commented Zero. "That's where the feast really happens—not only with the food but the fun games with people and all the loving afterward."

"And you get to see so many old friends," commented Sandra.

"And make new ones," affirmed Spot. "New friends arrive every day."

"How often do the games happen?" asked Dittims.

"There has never been a set time that I know of," said Spot in thought. "They get posted down at the community center garden well in advance to give everyone time to know about it. And of course, since we love them so much, word travels fast."

"Let's see what we have in the way of fruit today," inquired Munchkin. "Hmm, no figs, they are my newest favorite, but apples are always a good option. I remember one place where we lived before moving to Alabama that had apple trees in the backyard. I would pull the apples from the lower branches and eat them."

"Deer from the woods would also come down and eat those apples," reminded Ruth.

"Yea, that's how I found out about them. I would try to get to them before the deer. Then I would eat too many and then be sick for several days."

"As I recall," reminded Ruth, "you never were one much for moderation."

"And still isn't," teased Gypsy.

Chuckling as he finished his meal, Spot asked, "Do we want to go back to the gazebo or inside to continue?"

"If we go inside, I will get too comfortable and fall asleep," said Sam.

"You will probably fall asleep regardless," teased Ruth. "I vote for the gazebo. The air is refreshing, and if we get restless, we can take a walk through the maze."

"That's a good idea," agreed Spot. So after all had completed their meal, they turned back to the gazebo for more stories.

"There are quite a few of you here," commented Dittims as they got situated on the gazebo. "How long does this usually last? Not that I am complaining, I am fully enjoying myself but just curious."

"Well, it differs due to who is here and the stories that come to mind. Plus, interruptions always play into length of time it may take. Azer, you were the last to arrive before Dittims. How long was it for you?" asked Ruth.

"Not exactly sure, I didn't really count. There were extra things going on that distracted us from just story time. It may have lasted as long as two weeks or longer, but it was so interesting, and the love was so comforting that I didn't care. Some friends that are not here today came by with many stories and others that are here now, like Samson and Rusty, probably make each time different. It is just a great experience."

"Wow, I didn't realize it was such a process," said Dittims.

"It's not really a process, Dittims. We just want to give you as much knowledge about the past, present, and what to look forward to as we can," affirmed Ruth. "You will still be learning many interesting facts hundreds of sleeps from now about others, yourself, and about the Master's plan for you. People as well as other members that are not here today will get around to meeting you and filling you in on all sorts of details that they experienced. We are all interconnected way more than you realize, and it will take an eternity to even begin to figure it all out. It will be great, you will see." Affirming nods from all members made Dittims relax and ready to take in more story time.

"With that said," continued Ruth, "shall we continue with Nellie's stories?"

"Yes. We were talking about a beach trip, so let's talk about a story from home that, while funny to you guys as you have heard it before, was rather painful to me."

"Ah, the firecracker story," said Spot.

"Could have been a major explosion, for all I care," murmured Nellie.

"You know," commented Ruth, "not meaning to interrupt, but I don't understand why people like looking into the sky and watching it exploded. I remember Christy taking me to an outdoor celebration one night. There were lots of people there, and I got lots of extra love from people I didn't even know. Other dog people generally love petting someone else's dog, and I thought everything was great until all the explosions started. I almost climbed inside Christy's shirt. I was terrified. We even left early for my sake."

All the guys started laughing. "It's just not ya'lls thing," teased Rusty. "You ladies are just sensitive."

"Oh, I beg to differ, Rusty. I am a male hunting dog. I don't like loud bangs either," affirmed Spot. "There are a lot of us who don't care for loud noises."

"Well, Christy's aunt on her mom's side and her husband came down to visit during a special holiday that happened during the summer. They brought with them a bunch of firecrackers. Everyone knew I was scared of loud noises, but since we were all outside having a cookout, they forgot my fear or me even being there. Christy was still young at the time and was not fully aware herself of what a firecracker was.

"You remember the pasture Spot told you about that the horse was in? Well, the town had grown some by then, and farm-type animals were no longer allowed in the city limits, so Miss Priss was moved to the farm. The pasture became a nice grass field that was used by the neighborhood kids to play ball."

"Was it still fenced in?" asked Dittims.

"No, and that is where they were setting up the grill for a cookout. They also had metal sticks for the children to play with that had a gunpowder residue on them. When you lit them, bright sparks came off it until all the residue was burned off. Those were okay, no loud banging, and kind of fun to try to catch the sparks. Even though they were hot at first, the spark was gone by the time they hit the ground, and it was fun dancing through Christy's legs as she played with them."

Nellie sat still for a moment in memory.

"Then the noise started. The first one made me trip and fall on my face. I looked around trying to see what had happened when I saw her uncle throw something else toward the driveway. When it exploded, I took off for the door. Christy knew I was scared, so she ran after me. I desperately wanted inside away from the noise, so she opened the kitchen door to let me in. Now my bed was in the laundry room, in a basket by the dryer. I didn't always sleep there, but that was my designated area for cold or bad weather. So when Christy opened the kitchen door, I raced toward my sleep area, not really watching where I was going, only wanting my safe zone. Little did I know that someone had latched the laundry room door closed, so when I hit it at full speed, it went nowhere, and I got knocked back into the dining room on my haunches with my head seeming to spin in circles…saw my own stars at that point."

"Oh no," choked Dittims, trying not to laugh out loud, while the others were lying down in full laughter. "Were you hurt?"

"Christy heard me hit and came running from the kitchen. My head was sore, but I was not seriously hurt. She realized what I had done, and trying not to laugh herself, she picked me up and checked me out. Then we went to cuddle on the sofa. My head hurt for two days after that."

"Fear can make you do some crazy things," affirmed Ruth.

"I always said," continued Nellie, "it was that knock in the head that made me fall for Rascal. I meet him about a month later and thought I was in heaven. Next thing I know, I have Sandra, Trip, Tiny, Little Spot, and there were four others that did not make it. They were just too small because I am an awfully small mom to have that many babies at one time. The older daughter, CJ, help me to keep them feed as I did not have the strength or food supply. When they had grown and were ready for new homes, Sandra stayed with the family. Trip went down to friends at the end of the block where they had twin boys, so Trip's energy was a good thing for that family. Tiny went to friends across town, and Little Spot went out to the farm where I was born. He was the guard of the henhouse and was very good at his job. He ran off a fox once and killed a snake that was headed for an egg dinner."

"Yuck." Several of the team shuddered.

"New story please, to get that vision out of my head," said Ruth.

"Okay, then lets tell a story of adventure in the area near the home, over by Pine Needle Hill. It could have had dire consequences except for my smallness. It's my only sort of hero story. I know that others of y'all may have a true hero story, but this one is about as close as I got."

Chapter 8

*The greatest gift an animal has to offer
is a reminder of who we really are.*

Nellie resettled on her cushion and started again. "The next street over from the front of the house was the access road that had the new construction of the elementary school on one end, and the firehouse was sort of in the middle of that road. Behind the firehouse was a large wooded lot full of pine trees with a large knoll that had many bike paths leading from hilltop down to the large open field. The kids in the area had named this knoll Pine Needle Hill. Across from Pine Needle Hill in the next block toward the school was the old baseball field. The new hospital construction is next to both of these fields in the next block down."

"Were these blocks large?" asked Dittims. "Sounds far for a smaller child."

"I would not say so, about two houses deep. The houses would be back to back with fronts facing their own street."

"Plus in that era," commented Spot, "people walked a lot, so walking two blocks was no real distance."

"On breezy days," continued Nellie, "when no one much was on the hill were the times Christy and I would head over there and just sit on the ground under the trees and listen to the breeze move the trees creating a swishing moan and creaking sound as they swayed. From the hill, you could see traffic as it was heading north on the new main road. Or looking the other way from the hill, you could see the birds soar in the wind currents of the open ball field and rest in the openings of the old building. Back in the day, there had been a small professional ball team that played there. But now it was abandoned and left to decay."

"Christy found a kitten there once," remembered Sandra, "and took it home. But Mom said no and found it another home. Her mom did not like cats, something about its fur."

"But we have fur," reminded Rusty, "and I have a lot of it."

"It's different," explained Nellie, "fuzzier or something."

"I guess," resigned Rusty.

"There was one time that I remember more than the most," continued Nellie.

"There was an approaching hurricane in the Gulf of Mexico, and where those storms actually make landfall dictates the amount of rain that gets carried inland. This particular storm had rain clouds that stretched far inland in front of its center of destruction."

"Does that make a difference?" asked Dittims.

"Yes. It means a longer period of rain before the storm gets there."

"And if the storm is large," chimed in Sam, "you could have inches of extra rain."

"Christy and her brother had been fighting earlier that day as siblings sometimes do, but Christy's feelings had really been hurt. Her brother loved to play fireman, and he built an elaborate house out of a large cardboard box. He then took several things he thought were not used anymore and put them inside the box. In grabbing things to put in his hotel, he grabbed an old stuffed toy of Christy's. Now this stuffed toy was a favorite stuffed animal that was a gift from her grandmother. It was a red-and-gray elephant. She had named it Bobo."

"Oh," said Dittims, "I sense disaster coming."

"Then he drug the cardboard box into the center of the driveway and set it on fire, watching it burn while as he sprayed it with the water hose. After the box was burned up, he pushed the remaining unburned pieces to the side off the driveway for a later cleanup project. Christy went to investigate what he was doing and spotted the leg of her stuffed elephant."

"I knew this was going to be bad," said Dittims.

"I remember hearing her scream at him, not really understanding what the issue was, but then I saw the charred leg in her hand. She was so upset she ran off down the street. Later when she still had not returned, I began to worry. The rain from the storm was beginning to fall but was still very light. The family rule was to be home when the streetlights come on or if the weather turns bad, but still she did not show. Mom began to worry and was calling for her. She had asked Ben if he knew where she was, but he said no. She called around to the neighbors, but no one had seen her.

"By the time her father had gotten home from work, the sky was getting dark, and the storm edge was getting closer. The thunder was starting to be heard but was still a good distance out."

"Well, the only consolation I have," said Dittims, "is that I know she was okay because I got to be with her."

"Christy's father asked if anyone had let me go out to find her for her knowing the close connection we had and that maybe I might be able to find her. Mom made some remark about me not being Lassie and Christy not being Timmy in a well, but I had no clue as to what she was talking about. With all the walking we had done around the surrounding neighborhood, I did not remember ever seeing anything resembling a well. Her father changed clothes, and we went in the car looking for her. As he drove slowly through all the neighborhood streets, we neither saw nor heard anything while he called for her. He stopped at the fire station just to see if they had seen a little girl come by that area, and one of the firemen in the back had remembered seeing a child running up the hill of pine trees but did not recall if it was a girl or boy. He said he would help him look for her as he remembered which path the child had taken. So both men put on rain gear and walked out behind the firehouse to go look for her. I was not going to be left behind, so I tagged along as well, regardless of getting wet."

"So many things could have gone wrong," commented Ruth.

"After searching all paths, we still did not find her. Coming down from the hill and heading back toward the firehouse, Christy's father wondered aloud to the fireman if she may have gone to the old ball field stand to get out of the weather. So they headed over there. The fence was locked up, but there were plenty of room for a small child or me to scoot through. After a couple of calls, a weak and scared voice could be heard over the increasing storm, and I scooted inside and raced toward that voice as I knew it was Christy. I found her in a room that had a short wall on one side with another small room behind it. There were old and faded pictures of food on the walls, so this area must be where they had gotten snacks when the ball field was active. Christy was sitting in the corner away from the rain and wind as it blew through the large open spaces. The father and fireman had climbed over the fence to come in. The fireman had brought an extra raincoat and pulled it around Christy. Then we headed back toward the warmth of the firehouse. I even got a warm towel wrapped around me to help me dry off."

"Did she say why she did not go home?" asked Dittims.

"She said she was heading home when she heard the thunder and got scared so went to the ball field to get out of the storm."

"Those hurricanes can be vicious," commented Sam. "I remember more than one evacuation from the beach house when we were there with deputies coming by telling us the storm was getting too close and we needed to leave."

"Yes," said Dittims. "I remember when Hurricane Katrina hit New Orleans. It was a devastating time for that area and even up in the mainland near us. A lot of people came into our area to get away from that storm, and some lost their homes and business. Some even stayed in the area and started all over."

After a few thoughtful moments, Rusty asked Nellie what was the end result of her trip in the rain.

"Their father sat down with both of Ben and Christy and got to the root of the problem. He made them understand the dangers of the world and why you should never go out alone. He also fussed at them for not being respectful of each other and each other's things."

"From what I understand," commented Ruth, "as adults, Christy and Ben get along great, but as kids, they did not."

"I think that is typical," said Spot, "even in our realm, except I think it is opposite for us. We got along great when young, but then as adults, we can be…" Spot paused, searching for the right word.

"Territorial," said Zero. "I think humans call it jealousy."

"Yea," agreed Spot, "that's one emotion we don't ever have here. When we come here, we bring only the good characteristics we had, plus any creative thinking abilities we did not know we had. I love the arty-type traits that show up unexpectedly. All good characteristics come that are used to uplift and bring joy to anyone or anything. They show the love of this place. So much love, no one is ever left feeling short. It's the Master's way, and he will use all of that to blend us together for the good of all creation and his ultimate plan."

"Nellie, you and Sandra were obviously there at the same time. Was there ever conflict between the two of you?" asked Sam.

"No, during that time, we were very close to each other. Two of my other pups were relatively close by as well, so we would all go to visit each other and tell stories of what our lives were like at the time. Then as I got older, I started getting sick. Sandra was very helpful in taking care of me before it was my time to come here."

"Yes," affirmed Sandra, "I hated it when Mom got sick. I didn't want to lose her. I was always closer to her than I was to the human family, except of course Christy."

"I remember once when Christy got sick," continued Nellie, "CJ came and got both of us and took us to her room. With the parents' bedroom in back of the house, they did not hear if anyone got sick or was crying at night. CJ would always be the comforter, especially to Christy. She was ten years older and was a great friend. She even took Christy with her whenever she would go off with her friends. You know she is already here over in District 41 on Second Street. It's a lovely cream-colored brick house surrounded by azaleas and pine trees out front. Its circular driveway wraps around to the back and a big pool in the back. It's where Sugar lives."

"Oh yea," chimed in several members.

"Well then, Nellie, are there other particular stories you want to share, or are you ready for a break?" asked Spot.

"I think I am done for now. There will always be time for extra stories, remembrances, and similarities to stories being told. But let Sandra have a time for now. She can tell about her trophies."

"Trophies?" questioned Spot, looking over at Sandra. "I don't remember stories about trophies."

Sandra broke into laughter. "Trophy is a very vague term for what really happened, but I have a suggestion before we start. Why don't we take a break, stretch out legs, maybe walk through the front part of the maze? Blacky was telling me the sasanqua and double pink camellias are in full bloom on the front side."

"Oh," agreed Ruth, "that sounds like a wonderful plan."

"You girls just like smelling the flowers," teased Zero.

"And you guys like taking breaks to go play with the fish down in the creek," came back Nellie, teasing with Zero.

All the guys nodded their heads knowing this was in fact the truth. So they all headed toward the front section of the maze.

Their entrance to the maze from their yard is an extended arbor. The arbor is draped with a mixture of purple-and-white wisteria blooms that hang gently through the openings. This resulted in a peaceful beauty with a fragrance that is so light you hardly notice it. Once through the arbor you could turn either right of left. The walkways in front of the first section of the maze were walled on either side by a short barberry hedge, a delightful evergreen shrub, which showed small bell-shaped flowers in clusters, resulting in bright red berries when blooms are gone. The hedge was broken periodically with other evergreen shrubs such as camellias of various colors, rosacea, commonly called the bride for its showy white clusters, fuchsia of various colors, and gardenias.

The maze itself was divided into three sections with each section having its distinctive type of vegetation. The first section is filled mostly with evergreen shrubs and various woody plants, some having beautiful flowers and some with edible fruits for wildlife. Most of these require little pruning and are therefore a great asset for the front section.

OUR HOME OF LOVE

The second section had no hedges but was open with flowering trees or shade trees and benches to sit and relax. Multiple clusters of flowering ground covers and other flowering vines surrounded the bases of the trees and gave extra color to the area.

The third section of the maze was the entrance to the large cut flower gardens that were also divided into sections for research and pollination programs with testing of new varieties of bulb flowers. The paths in this section were more straight-lined to carry you quickly to your area on interest. The last rows of this section were showy flowers deemed as the cut flowers to be taken inside for enjoyment. And deeper still through the maze were the orchards and vegetable gardens for all to use as something was always blooming or ready for picking.

Back at the front of the maze, the girls were admiring the few new bushes on the first leg that were in full bloom.

"These two bushes on this side are new to the maze," said Sandra. "Blacky was telling me that they had been grooming these for a manor on the other side of our area, but the owner really did not care for pink, so they swapped out a white for this pink. It really is lovely, isn't it? That one over there is a double petal, makes it look like a rose."

"I don't smell anything," commented Rusty as he leaned in to sniff the bloom.

"No, these don't have a fragrance," explained Sandra, "but there is one on the next leg that does, and it is called fragrant pink."

"Hmm," was all that Rusty could say.

"We know this is not ya'lls thing, but we appreciate you coming with us to look at these new arrivals," said Ruth.

"Hello, Ruth, y'all admiring our new additions?"

"Hey, Maryann. Guys, this is Maryann. She is one of the botanical researchers for developing of new hardwood varieties like the camellias. Yes, we just heard about these new additions and came to see them. They are lovely, aren't they?"

"Yes, they are, but actually, Gerald is the one responsible for this new variety."

"Really, I thought he was more into bulb flowers varieties."

"He usually is, but this was a request from his grandmother, and I think he did her proud."

"He did indeed," commented several of the girls while the guys just nodded appropriately.

"It was good seeing you all, got more things I need to get done. Take care."

"See you next time. Tell Gerald I said good job," said Ruth as Maryann headed on her way.

"Fun stuff," said Ruth, turning back to the team. "Shall we head back to the gazebo?"

They all nodded and turned back toward the gazebo for Sandra to begin her stories.

Chapter 9

> A dog's love can make even the
> worst day survivable.

Once they were all settled back on the gazebo, Sandra started with her stories.

"As you all know, Nellie is my mom, and bless his little pea-pickin heart, Trip is my brother. There are others of my siblings here, but they are in a different area. You can meet them, Dittims, possibly at the next game day. And as you can see, I am the same coloring as my mom, white with black spots, but of course, the spots are in different places. And I am also smaller that both mom and Trip as I was the runt of the litter. I think that is why the family kept me. Plus I was cute."

Soft loving chuckles flitted around the gazebo.

"While I am the smallest, I am also the fastest. My favorite memories with Christy were the garage races."

"Yes," agreed Nellie, "but I still do not understand why the two of you thought that was such fun. I would lie in the sun and watch you run back and forth like I was watching a tennis match."

"I know," snickered Sandra. "For those who may not be familiar at all with this made-up game, let me explain the full layout. As you recall from other conversations, the shape of the house was like a *T*.

The bottom of the *T* was the garage and the back door. The top of the *T* on the pasture side of the house was the kitchen and the most used door for going in and out of the house. What Christy would do was run to one of those doors while calling me to come there. I would race to that door, and there would be a treat on the step, usually a cheese cracker, but Christy would be gone. As I was eating the cracker, I would hear her call from the other door, so I would run to that door, to find again another cracker and no Christy. Where the fun came in is I would try to figure out which door she would go to next and try to beat her there. But she was sneaky and would go to the same door twice sometimes."

"What would happen if you got to the same door she was at?" asked Dittims.

"Oh, those were special," said Sandra with fond memories. "I would get two crackers and some loving. Those were the trophy moments. Not sure which was best, the two cheese crackers or the loving. There would always be extra crackers with the lots of loving when the game was over."

"Sounds like real special time, but I am curious," asked Dittims, "did you stay outside?"

"Most of us were considered outside dogs," confirmed Spot, "coming in only when the weather was bad or too cold, but every once in a while, Christy would sneak the smaller girls in to sleep with her."

"About the time that I came along," explained Sam, "the mindset of pets for people was beginning to change. Pets were becoming more wanted, and they were being kept inside. New breeds were being created by refining breeds or by mixing breeds to become a new breed. You, for instance, Dittims, are a good example of mixing two breeds to make a new breed. And there were generally reasons for the mixing, as with my breed, low to the ground hunter, long ears for holding in scent, extra skin, and so on."

"The working dogs, like most hunting breeds," chimed in Spot, "were still kept outside but better cared for, kept clean and dry in kennels, and were not made into pets. They were still loved, but they had a job to do and had to remain focused on their duties."

OUR HOME OF LOVE

"I guess I can really see how we are considered spoiled," commented Dittims. "I even had my own chair."

"And I remember why that was necessary," teased Munchkin.

"During the winter months, Mom and I shared a blanket in an old laundry basket next to the dryer. In the summer, we had access to the back porch to keep us out of the rain. I remember one summer was wetter than usual. Christy had an entire doll play area setup on the porch. There was a small electric stove, which actually belong to her sister Sarah, and a couple of makeshift doll beds made out of boxes and doll blankets. There was a small table and chairs and even a couple of small rocking chairs—probably one of the same chairs Christy used to climb up by the TV and fell off when a toddler."

"I stayed on the porch a lot that year. Mom had already come here, and I was missing her terribly. Christy would let me curl up in one of the doll beds. It was a tight fit but softer than the concrete floor and dry from the weather. There was a tall hedge along the length of the porch that blocked the rain and wind from gaining access to the porch."

"That sounds like the place to be all the time," commented Rusty. "I actually had my own house and fenced-in area to keep me dry and safe."

"You would think that but not really," said Sandra. "The grassy area outside the kitchen got warm sunshine most of the day, and it was my favorite place. There had been a rose garden there once, but the roses had died, and extra hay had been placed over the area, making a soft place to lie. There would even be times when Christy would bring out a blanket, and some dolls or a book and would lay on the blanket. I was always the first on the blanket when she got it set. We would even take naps together sometimes. Now that was some good sleeping."

Chuckles and memories flooded each member as they thought back on some good snuggling times they had had as well.

"Let me tell you about our farm trips," continued Sandra. "Remember Mom explaining how one of my brothers went out to the farm where she was born, Little Spot. Well, this farm belonged to the Christy's grandparents on her mom's side. They grew tobacco as a main stay but also grew sugar cane, corn, okra, and various beans for themselves and family members. They even had a few pigs which are stories for another day. The grandfather did not run the farm by himself but had a foreman, and this foreman and his family took care of things. We would go sometimes on Sundays to check things out. I liked visiting with Little Spot, but my favorite place on the farm was the clay pit."

"I haven't heard you speak of the clay pit in some time," said Gypsy. "The pit was pretty much gone by the time I came along, but I did enjoy the farm trips as well."

"That area of the south," explained Sandra, "has an under soil called red clay—noted as South Georgia Red Clay. It will mess up any clothing a person has because the red rusty color never fully comes out of clothing when washed. There was a stretch of land the farm did not use because of the high amount clay. Plus it was on the back sections of the farm. There was a big highway going in around that stretch of the state that went from the end of Florida to somewhere way up north maybe as far as Tennessee."

"That's not that far," teased Rusty.

"It was at that time, matter of fact, during this time it only reached to mid-Georgia, didn't even get to Atlanta yet. I remember Sunday afternoon trips the family would take on the completed sections of the highway to a motel in Tifton, about an hour's drive, just to buy ice cream from a motel restaurant. Anyway, the road construction company bought rights to the dirt, meaning they didn't buy the land but paid for using the dirt, so it made a huge hole in the ground, and we called it the clay pit. It was a great place to play."

"Christy, her brother, and I would just run up and down the slopes, sometimes falling and rolling down the hills. The grandparents would sit on the hood of the car and just watch us. They had water and a snack for us when we would get tired. I remember one time when we were heading up one slope that Christy caught sight of a coiled-up snake. She made a fast pivot turn to run away and ran straight into Ben, knocking him down, then both of them were tumbling down the hill. I was not aware of what was happening and thought we were just racing down the hill. When they got to the bottom, they excitedly told of the varmint they had seen, so the kids and their grandmother got in the car while Buck, their grandfather, checked it out. Sure enough, the snake was there, but he was dead, and since snakes don't have eyelids, he was still looking alive."

"Oh, those things are so horrible." Ruth shuddered. "I have had an encounter with one, Sandra has, and I think you have as well, Gypsy."

"Yes, I have," agreed Gypsy.

"And Christy had several encounters with them on her own," commented Sam.

"Remember, Ruth," said Munchkin, "I was with you when you had your encounter."

"Yea, but you didn't even see it until Rick killed it. You just jumped over it like it wasn't there." Ruth paused in memory for a moment. "It looked right at me."

Laughter and sympathetic understanding filled the gazebo.

"Okay, new subject," said Gypsy.

"But I do still want to talk about the farm some more. There were so many wonderful memories. So I think the sugarcane is a sweet memory to start on. In the summer, when the sugarcane would get ripe, they would cut the tall stalks down. Then you would peel off the outer bark, cut it into mouth-sized chunks. Then you would chew all the juices out of a plug before spitting it out. Christy would always share with me, and I would lick the sweetness off but didn't care much for chewing on it like some did. It was too stringy. Little Spot loved it, but he was raised on the farm and was more used to doing things like that.

"As the temperatures got cooler, they would strip large bunches of cane, cut it into chunks, and put it in a big metal pot with a grinding wheel inside it. The wheel was attached to a long pole that had a harness on it, and they would attach one of the farm mules in the harness. As he walked around the pot crushing all that cane, the juices would run off from that big pot into a small pot that had fire under it. The juices would cook down into thick sticky liquid called syrup and people would put it on biscuits and pancakes. It really was quite tasty that way."

"What other things were grown or made at the farm?" asked Dittims.

"Well," continued Sandra, "during the late spring and through the summer, as the vegetables would get ripe, they would sell some of them at the roadside stand that was at the end of the driveway. Anything extra got put in jars for use during the wintertime when nothing was growing. But tobacco was really the main crop for the farm which was not to eat, and it would have to get cured before it could be sold at the market."

"What was wrong with it that needed curing?" Dittims asked.

"Nothing. It is just a term they use to get the tobacco ready to sell. The big green leaves had to be dried out before they went to market, and that's what is meant by curing it. They tied the stems of the leaves in small bundles and drape them over long sticks so they hang in midair. The sticks are placed in slots that are made in the walls of the barn that went all the way up to the ceiling. The barns were very tall with heaters that make the barn very warm inside, and it dried out the leaves. I went with them once to market. I don't know how anybody knew what was going on as people would walk down each of the aisles of tobacco stacked on flat pallets, pick up a few leaves, smell it, and the talk numbers so fast. I could not tell you what was said."

"Well, I think it is silly that people want to make products to breathe in smoke," Spot said as he took in a big breath of fresh air. "Oh, what is that smell?" he lightly moaned.

"That's something with apples," chimed in Rusty, who was also sniffing the air. "I know there is a bakeoff coming up soon, and lots of new recipes are being tried. My Christy has been testing various fruit fritter recipes. It has been marvelous."

"Your Christy?" questioned Dittims. "Are all caretakers named Christy?"

"No, silly," teased Sandra. "It just so happens that both of these caretakers had similar first name. But they were not even originally from the same country."

"Yea," confirmed Rusty. "My Christy is actually Chris Ann, Christy for short, and she was originally from Greece. She and her husband came to America to start their own restaurant business. The food was always marvelous, and the restaurant did very well."

"Speaking of food," said Spot, "I am beginning to get snacky. How about one last story, Sandra, and then we can head down to the community center?"

"Well, I can tell a story as we walk there together if you want," said Sandra.

"That sounds like a good idea," agreed Spot. "They are supposed to be having a community seed-spitting contest today, and I do love a slice or two of cold watermelon fresh from the creek."

"What's a seed-spitting contest?" asked Dittims.

"Watermelons," explained Ruth, "have large flat slippery seeds. And people like to have contest to see who can spit them the furthest. It's kind of silly to me, but they have fun with it, and the watermelon is always ice-cold where they were sitting in the creek behind the community center."

"I have had watermelon before but don't remember if I really like it or not. It's been awhile," commented Dittims as they gathered together to head down to the center.

"You will love it," affirmed Munchkin.

They all agreed as they walked together down the sidewalk.

Chapter 10

Dogs have a way of finding the people who need them the most.

"Let's see, since we have talked enough about the farm for now, let's bring it closer to home and talk about the storm drain," expressed Sandra.

"Storm drain? That sounds scary and dirty," commented Dittims.

"I didn't think it was that dirty. It was mostly for over flow from rainwater that would run through them during heavy rains or bad storms. There really is nothing quite equal to a South Georgia thunderstorm," explained Sandra. "They come up quick. The sky turns black as night, making all the streetlights come on, and you cannot see across the street with the amount of rain that can be dumped in a short amount of time. All of us in this group are spoiled with wonderful caretakers, keeping us out of bad weather. I have friends on the other side of the complex that had been homeless creatures. Their stories would make you shudder."

Affirmative nods from all team members knowing they, too, had friends who had not been as lucky as those in the group.

"The drains consisted of large concrete pipes that ran under ground to carry off the water from these storms and empty them into some of the creeks that were in the area. The creeks run toward the west side of town and dump into the Withlacoochee River, which then merges into the Suwanee River in Florida and eventually flows into the Gulf of Mexico."

"Wow," commented Zero, "don't think I have ever heard all of that before. How many miles of river are we talking about, and not to be sarcastic, but how do you know that information?"

Sandra laughed. "True, that it is not the type of information we normally have, but Christy had to do a school project on that river, and I listened to all the information as she read it out loud while practicing as she placed the information on her big posted board display. The Withlacoochee is about a hundred and eighteen miles long and dumps into the Suwannee River in Florida at the Suwanee Park Preserve area. That is a really nice place to visit as well, and I have a great story about that place for another day.

"Oh, we have gotten so offtrack. Okay, you remember the firehouse is on the same block section as home but one street north. One of the larger drain systems for that area ran from under the fire station. Then in the next lot over from the fire station, it ran through a large open ditch, which all that area had, at one time, been the small creek. The far side of the ditch connects into another concrete drain system that ran all the way under the elementary school that was the next block over from the empty lot. The kids would climb down into the ditch and enter this drain system to be able to walk under the school. Evidently, this was great fun as a lot of them did it. For a smaller child, the pipes were large enough to walk through without them having to bend over much. One day, Christy and I walked down to the school to play on the new swings at the school. The school had been completed and had a great jungle gym and lots of swings. She had noticed the larger kids go in and out of the drain in the past, and even though she had been told to not go in them, her curiosity had gotten the best of her. There had not been any rain in several weeks, so she knew the drains would probably be dry. So she decided to see just a little of it."

"Not good," moaned Dittims.

"As she entered the drain, I refused to go with her, but she picked me up and took me, anyway. It wasn't that bad, as you could see light through the system from the various grates stationed to catch the runoff from the rain. As we approached the first grate, she realized it was the grate in the center of playground where the water drained off from around the swings to keep the playground from puddling. In glancing further down the drain, it broke off into branches, and there was light further down from the other grates on the large playground as it wrapped around the school. She had no interest in going any deeper and had turned around to leave when she heard angered voices above. Christy stopped to listen, and after a few minutes, they walked away, so she turned to head on out of the drain. A sound behind her made her turn around and look back toward where the light from the grate at the playground was shining. Someone had dropped something down through the grate. She went over to see what was dropped. Lying in a shallow puddle of water was a small black cloth bag with a drawstring. Christy picked up the bag, opened it, and found a very sparkly necklace. She knew they must have dropped it by accident, so she tried to get out of the drain as fast as she could to catch them and let them know that she found what they had dropped. Once out of the ditch, she saw no one anywhere on the playground. She knew she needed to get it back to the rightful owner, and she knew when she told her mom the story, she was going to be in trouble for being in the drain. So when she told her mom, yes, she was in trouble, but her mom was thankful she had told her the truth. When looking into the bag, her mom got real quiet and asked her again to repeat her story. When Christy got through, she was sent to her room and told to stay there until called. I, of course, went with her, and we snuggled on the bed together. Sometime later, there was a light knock on the door. And two police officers, her mom, and her dad came into her room. Christy, at this point, was terrified, thinking she was in real trouble for getting into the drain. But after telling her story again and being asked questions about the voices she heard, they thanked her and left."

"That's weird," said Dittims. "What did they say?"

OUR HOME OF LOVE

"Evidently, there had been a jewelry store robbery, and that was one of the necklaces that had been stolen. About a week or so later, the owner of the store came by and gave Christy a crisp new twenty-dollar bill as a reward for being honest and returning the necklace. That was a great day as we both got to go to the ice cream shop, and I even got to have some."

"Did she still get punished?" asked Dittims.

"Not really," continued Sandra, "but she got a stern talking to about going into the drain, and I don't think she ever went in it again."

"There is the center just ahead," said Ruth. "Dittims, you will probably meet people and pet friends associated with Christy's past. I know Muffin will be there, as well as her caretaker, which is Christy's mom. She is usually always around when watermelon is being served."

The community centers were centrally located at the beginning of each district for ease of access not only within the district but also easily found by those coming from other districts. The seed-spitting event held by District 51 was favorite visited by friends of several other districts.

Dittims was surprised at the number of people and dogs that were in attendance. Many watermelons were sliced and scattered on ice across some of the tables. People were sitting in lawn chairs, leaning on tables, and standing in groups all in full heartfelt conversations. No one person was alone. The stage was set up with a measuring device to check distances of spit seeds. Grills were being set up, and the smell of fresh roasted corn filled the air. There were large bowls of potato salad, as well as platters of sliced tomatoes, fresh baked breads, and various raw vegetables that had been brought and laid out on other tables for all to sample.

As they entered the center grounds, Spot excused himself to visit his caretaker, who was busy at the grill. There was a gentleman at the center of the stage getting everyone's attention to explain about the afternoon festivities before everyone got too involved in cooking and playing.

"For those who are new to our fun event, welcome. We are glad you are here. We try to do this often to visit with each other, to be thankful for all we have, and events like this are different and fun. John, over there in the yellow shirt, is the current champion from the last time and is looking to be bested this afternoon. So before we begin to have too much fun, let us pause for a moment and give thanks for all we have, this wonderful feast, for being here and for the love of our Creator.

"Dear Father and Lord, as Psalm 148 reminds us, let all creation praise you regardless of who we are, where we are, or what we are. You alone have created us all great and small, and we thank you and praise you for all you have done and are still doing for us. Guide us each day to further your purpose for us in what we do. Amen.

"Let's all enjoy each other," he finished as he came down from the stage and headed over to some of his friends.

"Hey, there is my hero." A small white poodle walked up to Sam and gave her a gentle bump.

"Hey, Sugar. How are you doing?" asked Sam.

"Doing well, already eating. You know we always get here early to help set up."

"Hero?" inquired Dittims.

"Sugar," introduced Sam, "this is our newest member, Junior. He really goes by Dittims."

"Wow, you are a big one. I know Christy liked the larger breeds, but you are really big. It's great to meet you. And yes," she continued," Sam is my hero. Back in the day, there was a large German shepherd that was roughing me up a bit, and Sam, with her deep barrel-chested growl and bark scared him off and then chased him out of the yard and halfway down the street."

"I do have my moments," commented Sam.

"Yea, we don't see those much anymore," teased Zero.

"Were you hurt?" asked Dittims. "And are you part of our love team?"

"I was rolled a bit, more dirty than hurt. I am what you call an extended member as I belong to CJ, over there in the plaid shorts, helping with the grilling."

"Oh," remembered Dittims, "that's Christy's sister."

OUR HOME OF LOVE

"Yes, she is. Oh, I see fresh corn coming off the grill. That's my cue to help. I will try to visit more later," said Sugar as she was leaving. "It was nice to meeting you. Y'all must come over sometime. CJ loved horses, and you will fit right in."

"Thanks." Dittims chuckled.

"Okay," said Sam. "I am going to go over there to see Muffin. That's Christy's mom, and it looks like they are grilling tomatoes with cheese… So yummy. She adds some kind of special spice to them that really is good."

As Sam walked off, Spot walked back to the group, bringing friends.

"Hey, guys, I brought over a few canine companions of some of Christy's friends. You see, Dittims," Spot explained, "we are all interconnected, and as we make new friends, we begin to realize that sometimes our caretakers know each other.

"This beauty here is Lassie. She belonged to a coworker of Christy's down in Alabama. His name is Brian. This sheltie is Samwise, and he belonged to Carol, another friend of Christy's in Alabama. Now," continued Spot as he introduced the two remaining friends he had brought over, "this Boston terrier, Bugsy, and the Westie, Buddy, belonged to friends of Christy as she was growing up. Like you, none of their caretakers are here yet, so they visit with everyone like we do when events are going on."

"This is so fascinating," remarked Dittims. "It's all so new yet feels familiar at the same time."

"It's nice meeting you, Dittims," said Lassie. "We can chat more later, but right now, some of us have some duties to do."

"Thank you for coming over," said Dittims as they walk back to the grilling area.

"Let's head over to that small knoll over there," said Ruth. "We can see the contest from there, and they have laid out various vegetables, as well as watermelon on that table."

"Good idea, oh, and here comes some roasted corn," Gypsy said. So the group went together to stretch out and review the fun.

As Dittims was surveying his surrounding, his eyes feel on the fun groups in the center that were throwing the Frisbee with their canine friends and others guys throwing footballs with other guys.

"Is this considered a game festival that you were speaking of earlier?" he asked.

"No, that will be a structured gaming event with teams. This is just relaxing and enjoying each other," explained Zero.

"Sure is lots to understand, but it seems like I kind of already know some of it. I just need to get it in order."

"You will get there soon," said Spot, "Remember God created all things and said they were good. Maybe we need to show you the other side of the sector to get even a more different perspective. Why don't you and I go for a hike soon?"

"Oh," piped up Sandra, "can I go? I bet you are going to go see Leo. I have not seen his sister in a while."

"Sure, now is as good a time as any to introduce Dittims to the wild side. Got any other takers?" asked Spot, looking over the group.

"Really." Sam sighed sarcastically as she bit into another piece of melon.

"Well, we will discuss it more later," snickered Spot as he nudged Dittims affectionately.

Chapter 11

*The treatment of animals reflects
the character of your soul.*

"I believe that was some of the best food I have ever eaten. And, yes, I do love watermelon," said Dittims as they were coming back from the commons gathering. "I can remember trips being made to the local farmers markets, and while they were good, they were not as sweet and juicy as these."

"I think I hurt myself this time," moaned Zero.

"Well, if you and Rusty did not insist on having a watermelon-eating contest," teased Ruth, "you both would probably be feeling less stuffed."

"Oh, but it's so yummy," moaned Rusty.

As they got back, they decided the cushions of the floor inside the house would be more appealing than the benches of the gazebo.

"Explain to me again who Muffin was," asked Dittims of Ruth.

"Muffin was originally given to Christy's mom as a gift from her children. She is a basset beagle mix but looks more basset, just shorter ears. Christy's mom was a little older in age and was not doing well in housebreaking and other training aspects needed for puppies. After Muffin was a year old or so, her mom decided she just could not take care of her properly, and Christy said she would take her. Christy had her for about two years before she got sick and came here. She always was so happy and loved anyone who could speak with her and of course pet her."

"She is still that way," confirmed Munchkin. "She is usually one of the first ones down at any of the commons areas, where those she has loved have special events going on."

"Sandra, I believe you were in the storytelling spot. Do you have more to share?" asked Spot.

"Not for now. Why don't you take a turn at it, Gypsy?"

"Okay, Gypsy, you ready to give it a whirl?" asked Spot.

"Sure," she said as she got comfortable on her cushion. "To start off with, remember that I was fully grown by the time I was adopted by the family. A neighbor down the street from Christy's family was a veterinarian, and when my original caretakers had abandoned me when they moved, a neighbor friend had found me and took me by his office, hoping to find me a home. Sandra had come here several years before, so the family currently did not have a pet. The family had gotten into boating and was gone almost every weekend to the rivers in Florida, so it was not the best time to bring on a puppy. When the veterinarian spoke with Christy's father, he told him about me that I was grown, housebroken, and friendly. He just did not know what a scaredy-cat I was. Christy was in her preteen years and kind of a loner, so her father thought a pet would be a good idea."

Gypsy paused for a moment in memory.

"I remember the first time I saw Christy. Her parents had picked me up at the clinic and took me to meet her. She was visiting her grandparents at an apartment complex that they managed. I followed them as we walked up the sidewalk thinking this was going to be my new home, and Christy saw me right away, squealing in delight as she sat on the ground by me. We hugged and played for some time before it was time to leave and head to the family home."

"What were you a scaredy-cat about?" asked Dittims.

"Everything," teased almost everyone in the room at the same time.

"Not everything," defended Gypsy softly, "anything that quickly surprises me."

OUR HOME OF LOVE

"Like the hummingbird, last week," teased Munchkin.

"She was in my face."

"Hey, I can relate to that," agreed Dittims.

"Don't you worry about them, Gypsy. Remember, I am the knockout queen when it comes to getting scared," reminded Nellie.

Chuckles went around the room as all knew the teasing was good-natured for the bond in the room was strong for each member.

"Why don't you tell of some of the boating stories you got to go on?" encouraged Ruth.

"Yes, the trips to Florida were great fun. I apologize in advance, Ruth, but both stories that quickly came to mind involved snakes."

"Oh, good grief," moaned Ruth, "but this is a family that loves the outdoors, so it is what it is."

"The first story is about a fishing camp on the St. Johns River. It was a neat place with woods behind it and the river in front of it. There were walking trails winding along the edge of the water with small docks located along the path to fish from. They had a large dock where people could tie off their boats for resting from fishing or exploring trips along the river."

"Did they like fishing?" asked Dittims.

"Christy's family did not fish that much as they were playing on the boat with exploring sites along the river. The children were skiers, and they would ski behind the boat as it went down the river. I remember"—Gypsy chuckled remembering—"when they traded in their older boat for a new boat with two engines. Ben was out in the water, ready to ski, and when Christy's father hit the throttle for the engines, the extra power of two engines pulled Ben completely out of the water."

"Oh my," said Dittims. "Was he hurt?"

"No, but it was something to see. Then they throttled the boat down a bit. Christy never did learn to ski, but she loved to sit on the very front of the boat and dangle her feet over the bow, wrapping her arms over the railing that kept her from falling into the water. If the boat got into shallower water, she would be the lookout for logs and such that the boat might hit."

"I remember her stories of the dolphin that would swim right with the boat as they raced out into the gulf going fishing. She really loved the bow," Sam said.

"I preferred the back where the seats were on either side of the engines. I would usually be under one of those seats when we were moving or inside the cabin. I did enjoy the picnic stops, though, where we would park along the banks of the river. Some of the most beautiful wild azalea bushes bloomed along the edges of the river. They were light pink and had the sweetest fragrance. Christy's mom loved them, and they would cut limbs from them and bring them back to place in a makeshift vase when they got back to camp.

"When they built the house in Florida, they would go up river from there and gather those same flowers as well. She would place some in the living area and some on the dining table. The whole house smelled good."

"What was that camp like?" asked Dittims. "I remembered a church camp that was across the lake from the house in Alabama with a few cabins and a common eating area. I was told there was tent camping further back on the property, but I never went back there."

"Not really sure why they called this a camp. There were no tents but several family-sized cabins and two larger cabins for groups. There was a big dining area they called a mess hall, where everyone sat together at long tables to eat. They had some of the best little fried ball things. They called them hush puppies. They were made with cornmeal and had small pieces of onion and sometimes bits of bacon. They were so good.

"They called them hush puppies to shut the dogs up from barking when they were cooking outside," explained Sam. "At the Florida house, there were a lot of outside cooking parties after fishing trips, and one of the neighbors made what she called puppy drops, but they were sweet, and you dipped them in honey.

Well, at this camp, there was this rather large man that was the main cook, and on Saturday nights, there was always a big fish fry so everyone could meet one another. And he made onion and bacon hush puppies for the kids and dogs that were there.

"They also had a stout bulldog that lived there whose name was Bruiser. He was kind of protector for all the people there as he was the snake killer. Being on the river and having woods everywhere, you were bound to have a few around. If a snake was spotted, the owner would call him and say, 'Bruiser, snake,' and Bruiser would come running. He knew just how to come up on that varmint from behind to keep from getting bit, and he would grab it just behind the head and shake it until he broke its back. The camp's owner would then shoot it to make sure it was dead, then throw it deep in the woods to be food for other animals."

"Such a disgusting creature," commented Ruth as she shook her coat like she was getting rid of something crawling on her.

"I really only saw one in the few times we went there. But my favorite things we did on these trips were the various springs that we would visit because then I could periodically get out of the boat and visit."

"Oh, that sounds fun," said Rusty.

"It was nice. The Suwannee River had the better springs to me. There was a stretch of that river the family liked the best that had four springs right close to each other. Hart Springs was at the top end with Otter and Fanning in the center ending with Manatee Springs toward the bottom end of that group. Hart and Manatee were the family favorites for their boat accessibilities and the nice swimming facilities for the whole family. While the water was beautifully clear water, it was also freezing cold. When the kids got to the point of being beet red from cold, Mom would make them stay out a little while and warm up. I sat on the dock and watched. No way was I getting in the water."

"You would not even get in it if it was a warm spring," teased Rusty.

"You are probably right. Getting in water for fun is highly overrated in my book. But regardless, watching the fish that looked like they were just under the surface was interesting. They were a good five to ten feet deep, but it looked like you could touch them since the water was so clear. The deeper pools were set up for swimming, and some places had diving boards. The shallower areas were set up for smaller children as wading pools. Manatee even had a section just for pets. I was not interested, but I did walk over and speak with a few fellow canines about their trip. I met a quirky little Scottish terrier there that was all the way from Ireland. His family was on vacation in Florida for the entire summer break."

"Where did the family stay at the spring? Was a motel there, or did they sleep on the boat?" inquired Dittims. "I have seen some of the pictures of some of those boats, and some are huge with plenty of places to sleep."

"No, the boats you would see on those rivers were not that type of boat, and the springs were an easy day boat ride from several hotels along the river. Christy's family always stayed in same motel each time, which was a little bit up river from Hart Springs. It had a nice dock area to tie off several boats.

"Her mom would have picnic supplies packed for lunches, but breakfast and supper were always at restaurants, usually the one located at the motel. I remember one time Christy's mom was being very efficient and organized. She got all these new plastic storage bins for the dry food to help it stay dry and to keep from having to take it back and forth from hotel to boat. All the wet stuff or cold things went in the ice chest, and that had to be re-iced each day. The family came down to the boat one morning, and raccoons had gotten on the boat and eaten holes in the plastic containers to get at all the dry goods. They pretty much ate or ruined everything. So much for that picnic as they had to make other plans."

"Raccoons can be testy little critters," commented Dittims. "When we first moved to the Midwest, the rental house where we lived was on the edge of a state park, and raccoons lived in the massive oak trees on the property. In the middle of the night, they would start their ruckus, chattering and fussing at each other. I even had to have extra vaccines because of the pesky critters."

"I remember," added Sam, "when the boat types changed from the rivers boats to gulf-type boats. The size was a little larger, and usually, there was a door to the inside cabin to help keep any of the unwanted critters out."

"The gulf trips were after my time," continued Gypsy. "I was always on to the river trips. There was one river that was a family

OUR HOME OF LOVE

favorite due to its curviness, the Ocklawaha River. It is a main tributary for the St. Johns River. The Ocklawaha River's main source was a short five-mile river called Silver River, which came out of Silver Springs, a large spring that was an important tourist attraction for the area. They had glass bottom boats that you could see fish and other underwater things while riding in them. A little unnerving for me, kept worrying about falling in and getting wet."

Light chuckles and snickers went around the room as all knew Gypsy aversion to getting wet.

"Anyway, this river was shaped similar to the Blue Ridge Parkway that I have heard Zero talk about, only it was water."

"I am sorry, Gypsy. I don't know what the Blue Ridge Parkway is," said Dittims, a little confused.

"Oh yes, the Blue Ridge was in my time frame," piped up Zero. "The Blur Ridge Parkway is a winding road that runs along the sides of the Blue Ridge Mountains through North Carolina and up into Virginia. I think it goes all the way to Vermont, but the name changes along the way. It is very curvy."

"Yes," continued Gypsy, "and the Ocklawaha is just like that. It was only wide enough for two boats. The boaters would race up the river fast and zip around the river bends, splashing their wakes along the banks of the river. If you happened upon a fisherman, you slowed way down so as not to disturb his fishing too much. Christy's father would tie off the boat along the bank when they would stop for lunch and throw a life preserver in the water that was tied to a ski rope and then tied to the back of the boat. The children would jump in the river and have to come up quick to catch the life preserver and then pull back up the rope to get to the boat, then jump in and do it again. Since it was a main tributary for the St. Johns River, the current of the Ocklawaha was extremely fast, and if you missed the life preserver, it would be a hard swim or long walk back to the boat."

"Did you ever go in any of those rivers?" asked Dittims.

"I think we have already established that I don't do water."

Much laughter filled the room.

"There was one trip in particular that I remember as the day was warmer than usual. We had stopped for lunch under the shade of some low tree branches while Christy's mom was in the cabin making sandwiches. Her dad even sprayed the back end of the boat down with water from the river to help cool the floor off. As much as I didn't like getting wet, I did lay down in the coolness to help cool off. The children were doing their normal jumping in the water and floating downriver to cool off. One of the times when Christy was coming back into the boat, she screamed, 'Snake, Daddy, snake.' Well, that caused quite a stir. People in the boat were jumping on top of things, and Christy's mom banged her head as she tried to get up and run. She was deathly afraid of snakes."

"Yes, I feel her pain," agreed Ruth.

"Where was the snake?" asked Dittims.

"It was wrapped around part of the motor in the back. He was a long skinny green snake, just watching everyone as they were doing whatever, kind of minding his own business, not bothering anyone. When Christy explained where he was, her father caught sight of him and started laughing knowing it was just a harmless garter snake. He took the paddle and pushed it off the boat into the water, and he just swam away."

"While certain snakes may not be poisonous, they are all still harmful. If they won't actually cause the harm you may receive, you may harm yourself getting away from it," explained Ruth.

"Oh, that is so true," agreed several friends in the room.

"Hello, everyone," greeted Skeebo as he entered into the room.

"Skeebo, so good to see you," greeted Ruth. "How is the new common area project for District 62 coming?"

"It's going well, should be complete and ready for the big story time event that is coming."

"That's an event I don't want to miss," commented Spot.

"Should really be a blessing for us all," said Skeebo.

"And the cook-off afterward will be fabulous." Sam sighed.

"Is food always on your mind?" teased Spot.

"Could be." Sam chuckled as she plopped down on her pillow, and the room broke into gentle laughter.

"Pull up a cushion, Skeebo. Gypsy is telling some of her stories."

Chapter 12

Dogs have a way of filling an emptiness that we didn't even know we had.

"Got some stories, Gypsy, that do not involve our slithery friends?" teased Spot.

"Well, things changed as Christy grew older. She became interested in horses and started spending more time at the stable and less with me, but that shows the circle of life. I was getting on up in age and really just wanted to lay in the sun and sleep. She would get dropped off at the stable on Saturday morning and then ride her horse home for lunch. After lunch. she would ride back to the stable a different way for an afternoon ride."

"Would she ride by herself?" asked Dittims.

"She did a lot of the time but not always. There was one Saturday I remember more than most as I saw a catastrophe coming but was not able to warn her. Christy made a careless error of not paying attention of just how tall her horse was. After getting home for lunch, she watered her horse and decided to let him go into the field where Miss Priss used to be to eat some of the grass and clover that was growing."

"The fencing was gone by now, though, wasn't it?" asked Dittims.

"Yes, but there was a large pecan tree there that she could tie him off so that he could wander the length of his tethered line to graze. Her careless error came from her being a little lazy and not wanting to remove the saddle. So that combined with taking a shortcut under the old clothesline was a disaster waiting to explode, and it did. The increase in height from the saddle left no room for the horse to slide under the clothesline wire. When the saddle got caught on the wire, it pulled against the horse's girth and turned a calm placid horse into a terrified animal. He panicked and took off running. The clothesline was no match for his strength, and neither was the saddle, as the clothesline came crashing down with one pole, hitting Christy in the back and the saddle splitting in half lengthwise, landing upside down on the ground. Once the pressure from the saddle was gone, Cadet relaxed, settled down, and started to graze. Christy was not really hurt, bruised a little bit but mostly embarrassed from her lack of not paying attention."

"Oh my," exclaimed Dittims almost breathlessly. "What did she do?"

"She gathered Cadet's reigns and made sure he was okay. Then she tethered his lead to the tree. Now she had to go explain to her parents what she had done. The clothesline was toast with the post on that side broken off at the ground."

"Could they fix the clothesline?" asked Dittims.

"No. The post that broke was pretty rotten, and it was not really used anymore."

"What did her parents say?" asked Rusty.

"Well, her mom got a little excited as she was known to do with issues involving these large animals, but her dad just looked at her and said, 'Guess next time you will be a little more careful.'"

"That's amazing. How did she ride back to the stable without a saddle?" asked Rusty.

"Oh, that was not a problem," said Gypsy. "They all knew how to ride bareback. It just was dirtier because of the horse sweating and such. Her saddle was able to get fixed. It just took a couple of weeks."

"It's amazing no real damage was done," said Ruth.

OUR HOME OF LOVE

"I remember getting to go with her a few times when there was just cleaning that needed to get done for the horses. Several of the other riders would meet at the stable at the same time and muck out the stalls together. Then they would play or ride around the stable until their family members picked them up. I watched them in amazement as they would ride with no saddle or bridle, just using their legs to guide their horses. That worked fine until the horses got lazy and just wanted to graze. Then they would all come back to the tack room and tell stories of their rides with each other. Some stories were crazy, and some stories made me shiver with fear for these young carefree kids who did not understand where danger existed."

"Tell the story about the train," prompted Zero. "I sometimes wonder how young people make it to adulthood with the antics they pull as youth."

"I agree," said Ruth, shaking her head in agreement.

"Okay, but let's give a little background first. The stable was located at the end of a cul-de-sac that came through a growing subdivision. The land dropped down as it neared the stable, which placed it in the flood plain for the Withlacoochee River since it was just beyond the stable property. On the left side of the stable as you are looking at it from the road, there was a small creek that separated the stable and pasture from another subdivision on its southern side. This creek also flowed down and fed into the river. The riders would cross that creek and cut down the backside of that subdivision to get to a future subdivision that was nicknamed Snake Road due to the amount of snakes they had found when clearing the land. A lot of that area had pine trees, sage brush fields with occasional oak trees scattered through it. Since all the roads had been cut, it was a popular place for teens to race their cars and take their dates for evening drives. The roads were still red clay, but they were ready for paving once the time was right for the new high-end subdivision to get started. I think it was well over a hundred acres or probably a lot more since I really have no idea of size."

"Wow, that's a big area," commented Dittims.

"Yes, but the reason no building was being done was that it was an area of town that was not growing yet. It was coming because on the other side of that proposed development was the new area deemed for a large scale mall which also included external stores and restaurants. Plus the mall location was near the interstate, giving it easy access for local traffic and drawing shoppers as they headed to Florida. Near the proposed mall area on that side of the new sub-division development, there was an older stable with a much larger pasture area and was also a fun place for the riders to go. The riders from both stables enjoyed riding with each other through this new development and its many dirt roads."

"Once the development was built, did it destroy the places for the riders to take their horses?" asked Dittims.

"Probably, but it would be several years before they would even get started, and most of the current riders would have grown up and moved on to other things. It's the rule of progress, I guess."

"That shows that double-edged sword of progress, growth, and destruction at the same time," commented Zero. "So which part of the development was Christy's favorite?"

"The sides closest to her barn," continued Gypsy, "a little area she called the meadow that had a large log from and old oak tree that that had fallen. It was just the right size for her to sit on and let her horse graze. Remember I told you how the river ran close behind the stable property. The creek that ran behind the barn pooled just on the front edge of the new development behind the meadow, and then from there, it flowed further down to run into the Withlacoochee River. That pool from the creek was a favorite for the riders on those hot summer days. The horses stayed along the edges, though, and would kick up water from their front hooves to splash their bellies to help cool off. There was a set of railroad tracks next to this pool with a trestle crossing this section of wet land. Further downstream where the creek flowed into the main section of the river was another trestle. If riders were in the pool when the train went go by, they would wave at the train conductor. He seemed to look for them as he flew across this smaller trestle while it headed to the south side of town. The riders always knew if a train was close as they could hear the train whistle as it crossed the main river bridge about two miles further downstream. Now I do not know the full truth of this story, because I am telling it as I heard it from riders when stall cleaning was going on when I was allowed to visit. I just know the condition Christy was in for several days afterward to believe its worthiness."

"I don't know that I am familiar with this story, but this doesn't sound like it's a fun story," said Rusty.

"As I said earlier, the pool where they liked to cool off was right by that section of train track, and the pool was gotten to by a path that ran along side of the track all the way to the road where the road crossed from existing subdivision to new development. And the road went from pavement to dirt at the train crossing."

"So that I can visualize this in my head, the beginning of the new development, the meadow, and the pool were all right there together? Next to the tracks?" asked Dittims.

"Yes. Some of the riders were daredevils, and Christy was a big tomboy, not wanting to be shown up by any boy. The looming dare for the riders was that when you heard the train whistle as it crossed the main river bridge, you had less than two minutes to race down that path and cross over the track crossing before the train got there. There had always been joking about who would be first to try it, but no one had ever been there at the right time to give it a try. One particular day, Christy had finished cooling off and was just mounting back up to head back to the barn when they heard the first train whistle. Several had teased her into trying, so she cantered off, having no intention to try. Little did she or her horse know that a rattlesnake was just at the edge of the path. And when they got too close to the snake's liking, the rattles started shaking, filling the air with a frightening sound.

"Christy's horse bolted for home, zooming down that path at breakneck speed. She heard the whistle blow as the train was getting close to the small trestle by the pool, and she knew she may not have time to make the crossing before the train. Desperately, she began yanking on the reigns to stop this runaway horse, but there was no stopping it. She glanced back over her shoulder to see the train engineer frantically waving at her as he also realized the dire situation with his blaring whistle signaling the approaching of the road crossing. The beating of the hooves was matching the clacking of the wheels on the track as the engineer watched in horror. Tears were blurring Christy's eyes as she knew the severity of the situation. Her horse flew over the crossing with Christy glued to the saddle and hugging Cadet's neck in frantic fear."

"Thank goodness," whispered Dittims.

"The horse did not slow his pace until he was near the creek crossing that was just behind the barn and finally came to a full stop at the gate with the horse's sides heaving as they were both trying to catch their breath. Horse and rider were still shaking from fear with a full rush of adrenaline. Christy just sat quietly in the saddle at the gate for a few minutes collecting her thoughts before sliding off and opening the gate. As she led her horse into his stall, she noticed a deep gash on the side of his hip. Were they that close to getting killed, she thought? Or did they scrape something else as they raced in fear for home? I don't think she ever really knew or cared to know."

"Every time I hear that story, I get chills," said Ruth.

"For several days after that, Christy was very quiet. She would go to the barn but would not ride. She said it was because she wanted her horse to heal first, but I think it was a lot more than that. She spent a lot of time just grooming and loving on her horse."

"Did she get back on at a later time?" asked Dittims.

"Yes, but she changed her direction of ride," said Gypsy. "She would still go over to Snake Road from time to time with friends but never did go back to the pool. Sometimes, she would ride all the way to the country club, which was in the opposite direction, eat lunch at the canteen by the pool, and then ride back to the barn.

"The following summer, the family bought the property in Florida and built a vacation house. And the year after that, Christy and her brother both sold their horses to spend more weekends at the vacation house. Neither Christy nor her brother were ready to give up on their horses, but with the family spending more time in Florida, her father thought it was best."

"Did you get to spend time at the Florida house?" asked Dittims.

"No, I had already come here by the time the house was finished, but Sam did. I remember Sam coming along as a cute little thing, dragging her ears on the ground shortly before I got so sick.

OUR HOME OF LOVE

Christy's mom had always wanted a basset, and I think it was the dad that gave her a stuffed one that sat on top of the piano for years. And there was also a ceramic one that sat by the TV. I think he was thinking that no pets for a while since they were traveling to Florida almost every weekend."

"But that didn't work out like he had planned, did it, Sam?" teased Munchkin.

"No, it didn't," agreed Sam. "By that time, CJ had grown and was living in Florida. She had friends that bred bassets, so she got me for her mom as a gift. And while I was given to Christy's mom, I got lots of extra loving from Christy, so I have a dual home of sorts."

"So, Samantha," teased Spot using her full name, "are you ready for a turn at story time? Gypsy, I am not rushing you, am I? You sounded like you were winding down."

"Oh, I am good for now. Let Sam have a whirl at it next, but I suggest we take a break. Maybe resume tomorrow after a good rest."

"And I need to run on, anyway," said Rusty. "It has been great catching up, and I hope to hear more at a later date. I did speak with Dagu at the community center earlier, and he said he may drop by. So until next time. Take care."

"See you later," said Ruth. "We are having pancakes and fresh blueberries for breakfast tomorrow, and you are always welcome."

"I will see what I can do. Take care all, and welcome aboard, Dittims."

"Thank you, and hope to see you again soon. Maybe you can teach me all about Frisbee."

"Sounds like a plan. Brush up on your jumping skills. Bye."

"I think I may take a short stroll before quite time," Ruth said. "Since we don't really require as much sleep as before, although naps are always good, we use quiet time here, Dittims, to reflect on things as they are now, to focus on where we need to strengthen our thought processes, and to tune in more to the master's ways. And usually sleep goes with all of that."

"That sounds like a good plan," agreed Dittims. "Do you mind if I walk with you?"

"No, not at all. Thought I would go back down to the pond out front. There is a refreshing breeze blowing."

Once they were settled on one of the benches surrounding the small pond, Dittims quietly spoke. "Do you ever miss Christy?"

A soft chuckle came from Ruth as she started to speak. "This is one of the reason we are forever sharing the stories we have. Periodically, one will be told that someone in the group has not heard, and we laugh and enjoy the sharing time. We all miss her greatly but not in a sad way. We know one day we will all be together. And when that day comes, we will all meet her at the bridge and the fountain."

"The fountain where I came in?" asked Dittims.

"The fountain where we all came in," said Ruth, "man and beast alike. The Master will let us know when it is time, and we will all be there when she comes home."

"Wow, I did not realize that." Dittims sighed as he watched bees doing their evening foraging, moving among the flowers near the benches.

"Maybe sometime we can go over to the fountain to see what that would be like. Did you notice others coming across when you came?"

"Yes, but I was not sure what was happening and did not really pay attention."

"Yes, there is a lot to get used to at first. That is why we do the family review time. Once you get comfortable with all of us and familiar with how the house works, then you will start learning more about the workings of everything else. I have not been here a lot longer than you, so I still have lots to learn myself."

"I just hope I can remember it all," said Dittims, "and to not be absolutely blown away when I learn something new."

"I think that is what the Master wants for all of us," continued Ruth, "to know there is always an enjoyable experience, especially for his children, to ever learn of him, his love for us, and all of his mighty wonders. There are so many wonders still left for him to teach us."

Chapter 13

> While you may not change the world
> by saving one animal, you have saved
> the world of that one animal.

Dittims awoke feeling amazingly refreshed and full of wonder of all the things he experienced so far in his short time there. Others were still napping and quiet, so he wandered outside to enjoy the gardens. The humming birds were busy flitting among the trumpet vines by the gazebo, and a cluster of butterflies were hovering over a bush filled with tiny blue blooms near the back of the house. Since butterflies were a favorite of his, he walked over for a closer look.

"They are beautiful, aren't they?" came a familiar voice from behind as Munchkin came up beside him.

"Yes, they are," commented Dittims. "Do we always feel this refreshed after nap or quiet time?"

"Yes, it is different than before. We are more closely tuned in with everything here. We are more energetic, more loving, more enjoying, and just more at peace."

"There was so much excitement and amazement when I first arrived and wonderful stories with friends, and yet I am relaxed and comfortable all at the same time. It is wonderful how all of you have all made me feel. And the community center is another way to get to know even more friends."

A knowing nod came from Munchkin as she commented, "It is an amazing way that we all feel. The amount of love and peace we have here so far outweighs the pain that some of us went through before we get here. And it is even a stronger feeling for the humans. Members of this team were extremely lucky and blessed to have Christy and her family as our caretakers. From time to time, you will hear stories of those less fortunate but how they are truly at peace now and ever growing and showing more love than they thought possible of knowing. The Master has ways of placing all animal creatures with people who were never caretakers before and making new bonds that only increases the ever-growing love of this place. Come, let's go sit on the gazebo and enjoy the freshness of the day."

"And how is the replacement that is there now doing?" he asked. "Ruth was with the Master discussing her when I came."

"Ah, yes. Mimi." Munchkin paused a moment with a grin remembering the stories of Mimi and how it reminded her of herself when she was young. "Mimi was a rescue pup of about four months old. Her breed is coon-hound-black-lab mix with the energy of a Jack Russell terrier, which probably comes from her high-energy coon hound hunting side."

"I have heard others speak of rescues but not real sure what that means."

"Rescues are pets that either never had a home or for whatever reason no longer had a home. And there are centers that try to find them homes. As far as Mimi goes, I have a kindred spirit with her because she and I both have that high-energy level, but she is a lot smarter than I was. She is almost completely black except for a thin white streak on her chest, and she has very long legs. She has a good heart, but she has problems due to her abandonment or treatment as a pup, and it has affected her ability to bond well with Christy. She is slowly coming around but will probably not get all the way where she needs to be until she comes here.

"The story is that she was born in an extremely cold time of winter in an abandoned barn during a particularly cold winter with temps averaging around ten degrees at the height of the day and easily dropping into negative double digits at night. When the pups were found, she and her litter mates as well as the mom were taken to a nearby shelter."

"Do you not believe this story?" asked Dittims.

"I question it due to her fear of bonding. But at least the place where they were when Christy found them was warm and had food, but they did not receive the nurturing and love as some of us did when first born, so Mimi is not real sure what that concept is and therefore does not always respond as she should to be able to receive the love available.

"Christy has always been a fan of hound dogs as those breeds seem to generally be more loving and affectionate than some of the more exotic breeds. When she lost you, she was going to wait for a while to get another pet love but saw a picture of Mimi on a rescue website and knew she had to have you. She also knew that Lakota needed a companion because she had always had canine friends around her. Lakota's breed is a strong pack breed that needs that companionship."

"Yea," Dittims said.

"The shelter had named all the puppies of that litter after car types. I think Mimi's original name was Mercedes. Since Christy was not into cars and a firm believer in pets earning their names, she knew that name would not stick. Mimi was running free all over the lobby area of the shelter, and the people running the shelter wanted Christy to make sure Mimi was the one she wanted, encouraging her to look at all the pups. Christy knew from past experiences that could be a problem of her bringing them all home, so she refused to go look at the other pups.

"So with Mimi in possession, they headed for home. And the trip home was also interesting due to Mimi's energy and somewhat fear of riding in a car. Then, because some of us do not travel well, right as they turned and headed up the steep driveway, the entire contents of Mimi's stomach ended up in Christy's lap."

"Oh my." Dittims gasped. "What a mess."

"Well, fortunately for Christy, Mimi was not one to chew her food. Sometimes in kennel situations, you will see a lot dogs learn to eat very fast to assure they get food."

'Get what you can,' I guess.

"Yes, they have to learn to trust that food will always be available for them, and in some cases, they have to learn how to share knowing that there will always be enough for everyone. Fortunately for Christy, it had not been long since she had eaten, so it was mostly still whole and undigested, making for an easier clean up."

"Gross," Dittims chuckled.

"Indeed," agreed Munchkin. "The yard where they were living was fully fenced in, so that was a nice place for a dog to be able to run free without fear of traffic. So once they got home, that is where Mimi went until Christy could get herself and the car cleaned up. And"—Ruth chuckled—"this is where Mimi earned her name."

Puzzled, Dittims asked, "How did being in a fenced yard develop a name like Mimi?"

"Oh, it wasn't the yard. It was how she reacted to being put back outside in the cold and left alone. Her full name is Screaming Mimi, which was the nickname of a loud piece of German artillery during World War II. Christy's dad had been in WWII and told a lot of crazy stories that Christy had remembered. So when Christy placed Mimi in the backyard, closed the gate, and walked off, Mimi thought she was being put outside in the cold again and left like when she was tiny. So she began to scream in protest and fear of being abandoned. And goodness gracious, she was loud. A coon hound is known for its yippy bark, but Mimi's was more of a desperate scream than a yip."

"Does she still scream like that?" he asked.

"Not really, but it took several months for the trust to build. She now goes in and out as she requests because she feels safe knowing that all she has to do is ask, but," continued Munchkin, shaking her head, "if Christy gets out of view in the yard, she starts that high-pitched scream again."

"Does she think she is being left again?" asked Dittims.

"I don't think so. She is very protective of Christy and wants to make sure she can see her at all times. Since they are at a new house

OUR HOME OF LOVE

now without a fence, Mimi had to be placed in a chock collar…on a metal cable lead…that is attached to a concrete block that is buried in concrete in the ground."

Dittims burst in laughter. "Oh, my goodness, that's intense."

"Well, initially, when Mimi was still pretty young, she was attached with a small metal cable lead that was attached to the storm door of the front door of the house. This allowed Christy to let Mimi out and watch her without having to be outside herself. The problem with that is Mimi believes she is the family protector, and when she got older and full sized, she was very strong. One day, she saw a neighbor from next door that she knew walking down the sidewalk. Mimi wanted to go say hi and gave that cable a firm jerk and pulled the storm door off the front of the house."

"What?" exclaimed Dittims.

"Yea, so Christy took one to the large flower pots that was in the yard, the ones that are about three feet across and about three feet high, wrapped the lead around the bottom of the pot and then buried the pot halfway in the ground. After doing that, she planted flowers in it to add more weight. That worked for about six months until Mimi pulled the metal lead through the flowerpot by cutting it in half. She is such a strong dog."

"Is she dangerous?"

"Oh no, she is just very excitable. The few times she did break loose, she went over to who she was barking at and jump on them to visit. But she could accidently hurt someone, especially if it is a child."

"Amazing, but how is she with Christy?" inquired Dittims.

"Christy is getting on in age and does not have the strength or agility she once had, but Mimi loves her greatly. Christy just needs to get the yard fenced in so that Mimi does not trip and hurt her with that cable lead. She has already bruised her legs once with that lead being pulled against her leg when Mimi was on the chase. Once Mimi is better secured with a fence and no cable, she can then be the mighty protector she thinks she is. That is one reason we watch so closely, that and the crazy shenanigans that she pulls."

"That's amazing."

"She makes us giggle all the time, like the time she tried to bring a rather large limb into the house. Christy had been trimming an overgrown shrub in the yard, and some of the limbs were over six feet in length. Mimi, like most of us when we were young, loves sticks and tried to bring one of those limbs, fully covered in leaves, inside the house. But she could not figure out how to get it through the door. Christy just left the door open and watched her push and pull trying to figure it out. It was quite comical."

"Did she ever figure it out?"

"No. Christy went outside with her so she could have her stick and be close to Christy at the same time."

"I guess we all had our silly ways," mused Dittims, "some worse than others. Is Mimi slowing down some as she is getting older?"

"Some," said Ruth. "I think if you could have a fireplace going year around, she would probably always be calm."

"Why a fireplace?" asked Dittims.

"Only thing I can figure is with her being born at a very cold time of year, outside with no real way to get warm, when Christy turns on the gas fireplace, Mimi stops whatever she is doing and curls in front of it and sleeps regardless of hot she gets. They call it her pacifier."

"I don't think I have ever been in front of a fireplace until here," pondered Dittims.

"Me either, but I do remember Christy would burn off the leaves in the fall and sit outside with the fire until it was gone. I loved pulling out the pecans that were at the edge of the burn, and after they cooled, I would crack them open and eat the nut meat."

"How long were you with Christy?" asked Dittims.

"Not a long time. When I was a puppy, I was given by Christy as a gift to her youngest son. But when he could no longer keep me due to housing restrictions, I was given to the oldest son who had me for a couple of years, until he moved creating the same situation as the youngest son. So that is when I came to live with Christy. So I consider this my permanent home since I spent most of my time with her. Ruth was there as well, so we became good friends. Then

Christy's daughter came to live with us and brought her two dogs and two cats, so there was a virtual zoo of four dogs and three cats.

"Hello, there," called a voice from the patio.

"Hey, Spot," acknowledged Munchkin, "how are you this morning?"

"Hungry. Food will be coming up soon, and I thought I would hunt you two down."

"Oh, that sounds good," commented Dittims. "Now that I think about it, I am hungry as well."

"Sam was the only one still snoozing when I left." Spot chuckled. "But yummy smells from the kitchen usually always help her to fully come alive and get going."

"She does love her sleeping and her food," snickered Munchkin as they headed inside.

Chapter 14

> Have the heart of a lion, the skin of a
> rhino, and the soul of an angel.

"How did you rest, Dittims?" asked Spot as they settled on their cushions.

"Amazingly well," he said. "I was telling Munchkin that I was not sure if I was sleepy or exhausted from all I had done, but I was also so relaxed and at peace. It was kind of confusing. I was the first one up and didn't want to disturb anyone, so I went on outside. I have always been an early riser."

"I like being up early as well," mused Spot. "There is something refreshing about early morning walks, especially in the maze with all of its new and fresh smells."

"It helps me to get my focus in the right frame of mind," commented Ruth, coming out of the kitchen, licking her muzzle. "The chef was practicing again this morning," she said, defending the licking of her chops, "for the cook-off. I like being a taster for those new creations."

They all laughed as the smells from the kitchen were mouthwatering with a mix of breakfast fruits and the sweet fragrances of new recipes.

OUR HOME OF LOVE

"The pancakes are being placed in our bowls as we speak, so let's go ahead and give thanks before they are brought in," said Ruth as all lower their heads in thankfulness.

Warm pancakes with melted butter dripping down their sides and oozing with fresh blueberries were in each of their bowls. Complementing the pancakes were several scattered bowls of various fruits for sampling.

"Oh, these warm blueberries drizzled on top of these pancakes are amazing," moaned Dittims as purple marks stained the sides of his white muzzle as he devoured his pancakes.

"You are eating those like you had never tasted blueberries before," teased Munchkin.

Dittims sat quietly thinking about her statement. Then he walked over to where other bowls with various fruits and grains had been placed.

"Something wrong with your food, Dittims?" asked Spot, noticing his curious look.

"No, not at all. It just hit me that we never ate like this before. Why is it so different?"

"Because now we are different," reminded Spot as he went to stand by Dittims. "Think about the time span we all represent just in this room, and that is only a very tiny sample. The Master tells us we will all think different, be different, and eat different here. The lion will lay down with the lamb."

"Guess I just didn't think about it that way."

"I need to introduce you to some friends from the Back Forty, as we call it. It will give you an even larger perspective of how really different things are here."

"Those blueberries on the pancakes may have really been special to you, Dittims, but I was more partial to those warm apples in cinnamon," commented Munchkin as she resettled on her cushion. "They were delicious. Apples are probably my favorite thing."

"As I recall," commented Ruth, "the apple trees in the backyard were usually picked by you before Christy could get to the lower limbs."

"Me and the deer, that's how I found out they were so good. I saw the deer eating them, so I tried one, and they were right."

"Now that we are finished with our meal, are we ready to get going again? When we left off last time, I believe it was Samantha's turn for storytelling," said Ruth as she situated herself on her cushion.

"I think now may be a good time to take Dittims on a tour of the other side of the maze," said Spot, looking at Dittims for approval.

"Sure," he said, "is that the Back Forty that you were talking about?"

"Yes. It's a walk on the wild side," answered Sam, "and I have no interest in tagging along. But tell Leo I said hi."

Other noninterest came from the girls in his response to get others to go. As Ruth chuckled, she said, "Looks like it is only you guys that are up for a hike. Us girls will relax and enjoy the garden."

Sandra commented as she came in the room from the kitchen, "I still would like to go if you will not get way ahead of me. You're gonna go see Leo, right?"

Spot smiled at her. "You know me too well, little one."

"Been around you awhile, and I pay attention. Plus I like Leo's sister. She and I outsmarted all of the guys in the maze hunt three picnics ago."

"Yes, you did, and yes, we will walk slowly for you," teased Spot, "or we can put you on Dittims back, and you can ride."

"Oh, y'all hush and come on," she said with teasing disgust as she turned and headed out of the room ahead of them.

So Spot, Zero, Dittims, Skeebo, and little Sandra headed out for what was locally known as the Back Forty, which was located on far side of the maze. This area had fewer human inhabitants as it is where the large animal creations considered as wild animals lived and was a decent distant away from the main sections of houses, so it required some hiking. But moving about in heaven was totally different with large distances being easily covered in short amounts of time.

The scenery started changing once they got past the maze and the orchards. Tall savannah grasses covered the plains with large watering holes for all the animals and birds to drink from. The air was a little warmer, but the breeze kept it from being uncomfortable. There were wide paths through the grasses, or else Sandra would have been lost from sight. As they topped a hill, the sight below them was breathtaking. The tall grass gave way to a valley of bright meadows with picturesque umbrella thorn acacia and oaks trees scattered across the land. A wide meandering stream ran through the middle of the valley, and a few cottages were dotted along its edges. On one side of the valley, the rolling pasture was dotted with zebras grazing alongside gazelle and other types of deer species. As they neared the stream, what seemed to be large boulders in the distance were actually hippos warming on the edge of the stream. Dittims was wide-eyed as he took it all in.

"How you faring, Sandra?" asked Spot as they walked through the zebra while they grazed.

"I am doing fine. My size is tiny, but my energy level is mighty."

A loud roar froze Dittims in his tracks.

"Leo," called Spot as they turned in the direction of the sound. "How's it going?"

"Good, and you? Who is your new friend?" he said as they came together near a large acacia tree.

"Leo, this is Dittims. He is our newest member of the house at 904-TC4."

"Hi," said Dittims tentatively. "Sorry for staring, but I have never seen a lion except on TV, and y'all were kind of scary."

A loud boisterous laugh came from Leo, helping Dittims to relax and realize everything was okay.

"If I scare you, then you better get prepared for the LCs near the city." Leo chuckled. "But you will get used to it all here soon. You are a pretty big guy to be so cautious. You must have had an abusive life."

"Not at all," began Dittims. "My caretaker was very gentle. I had disabilities, which is probably where my cautious nature originated from."

"Is Elsa around Leo?" asked Sandra.

"Oh, hey, Sandra, I didn't see your tiny little self, standing behind this big guy. Yea, Elsa is down by Jantel's cottage. They are playing that game with colored rocks. You know the way?"

"Sure, I am going to zip down and say hi. Don't leave without me. I don't want to walk home by myself."

"We will visit for a while," assured Spot. "Take your time."

Sandra headed down toward the cottages as the guys moved further up the hill toward a larger oak tree to enjoy the view of the valley below.

"Dittims was curious about food here and how different it was as we are all vegetarians now," explained Zero.

"Well," explained Leo, "it is even more different on this side of the maze. Have you noticed the change in your body, Dittims?"

"No." Dittims paused, looking at himself. "I don't really see anything different much, but then again, I have full vision now that I didn't have before."

"Remember what you saw on TV about lions and their large pointed teeth? They are different now," Leo explained as he opened his mouth to show Dittims his squared-off teeth. "See, our teeth are flat and square for chewing grasses and vegetation, like a horse or cow. This was originally how the Master had it planned, but in Eden, all that changed when sin entered the world. Then the Master had to make a lot of changes for survival in a fallen world. Your teeth have been changed as well, but you may not have noticed it much because you may eat some of the same vegetables that people ate before coming here. The foods we have here are even more different than yours to accommodate what naturally grows in our region. More broad leaf grasses, large leafy vegetables, grains, milk, some fruits, and occasional cheeses that periodically get shared with us by the people that live here. When they are having the baking contest, we do partake in that. That's about the only time we really eat breads, especially sweet breads with fruit in them."

"There is one coming up from what I understand," said Dittims.

"Dittims," asked Spot, "remember the large flat area with the benches and the various covered table areas that we saw as we left the maze area?"

"Yea, I though it odd as it seemed out from everywhere."

"Actually, it's kind of a center area for this sector. When the Master is having a special meeting including man and beast together,

OUR HOME OF LOVE

that is where we meet. It's big enough for all of us with room for growth as needed. And it is wide and accessible through all districts."

Leo chuckled. "Dude, you just got here. You will be amazed with what the Master has planned for us. I am still learning, and I have been here a long time."

As they enjoyed conversation amongst themselves, an impressively large lion with black mixed in his equally large mane ambled by with a few other average-sized lions with him. Leo gave him a knowing nod as they headed to the other side of the stream.

"That's a big lion," commented Zero.

"That's Amra. He was one of the lions with the Master in the den with Daniel," explained Leo admiringly.

"The 'Daniel,'" whispered Zero.

Leo just nodded in affirmation. "Othniel, one of the other lions of that group, lives just downstream. They like to meander through the tropical forest on the other side of those hills there. Now, that is an amazing place to take Dittims to sometime. It has the most amazing waterfalls and totally different types of small animals."

"Wow," was all that Zero and Skeebo could say.

"Even here," explained Leo, "there are many varied stories that involve man and beast that you will come here to listen to Dittims. Some involve the Master, but most are amazing analogies of how the original plan was supposed to work. Some are how we are learning to get back to the original plan and creating the forever kingdom here."

As they rested and enjoyed the view, they saw Sandra returning along with Leo's sister. They chatted for a while, and then it was time they headed back home. As they crested back over the hill above the pastures, Dittims remembered something Leo had said. "What are LCs?" he asked.

"Whaaat?" asked Sandra in amazement that he knew the term.

"Leo said something about LCs, that I may be scared of them?"

"Fear is not the right emotion you will have. More shock and unbelief than anything," explained Zero.

"Oh, you will believe it," assured Spot. "When it is time for going into his city, we will explain about those then. You are just a little too new to wrap your head around those yet."

As they came back through the arbor from the maze to the back of the yard, they saw large bowls of steaming goodness being laid out for the latter meal of the day.

"Just in time, guys. We have already blessed the food," called Ruth. "How was the walk and visit?" she asked as they came onto the patio.

"Amazing," was all Dittims could say.

"I got to play Mancala with Jantel and Elsa," explained Sandra as she dove into a bowl of ripe juicy figs.

After the meal and conversations about the afternoon walk, Spot spoke his goodbyes. "I think everyone is well enough acquainted for me to take my leave for a bit. I have a few things I need to help my caretaker with in getting prepared for a new outdoor grill he is going to build."

"Thank you for the walk today and for all that you have helped me with in getting settled," said Dittims.

"It's what we do. I will stop by for more stories later. Take care."

After he left, they retired on their cushions for the evening rest. As Dittims settled on his cushion, he commented, "If we are all vegetarians now, why would you build an outside grill?"

"Are you kidding me?" Sam said just before nodding off to sleep. "Did you not sample those grilled tomatoes with cheese when down at the community center? Oh, and that hard crusty bread sliced thick grilled just right then smothered in honey or PB and J. Oh, and then there was grilled fritters and…z-z-z-z." And with those final thoughts, Sam fell into a full bellied restful sleep. The rest of the group enjoyed their thoughts of another wonderful day as they closed their eyes to quiet and blissful communication with the Master.

Chapter 15

Dogs are family, and family is forever.

Dittims woke before the others and was heading down the hall to the library so he would not disturb those still asleep. Ruth was coming out of the kitchen, and they met in the hallway.

"Good morning. Did you sleep well?" asked Ruth.

"Yes, I did. I thought I would go down and see the library so others could continue to rest."

"The library is a favorite reflection of her," explained Ruth, "not only because of the books she likes to read but the ability for her to paint, and the creative craft corner is in there as well. Those are the quiet things she enjoys doing."

"Oh, really?" said Dittims as they walked together toward the library entrance. "I guess I did not realize her interest in art," he said, pausing in memory. "Well, I should have, from the clowning ministry and face painting that she did as that is a form of art in itself. I placed those antics toward the love she had toward children."

As they entered the room, the smell of the flowers from the open windows filled the room. Dittims noticed an easel and table were next to the windows that he did not see when he first arrived and inspected the room. The easel was set perfectly to catch light as it came in from the windows, and the table was filled with various tubes of paints and brushes. Against the wall to the left of the door was another table piled with baskets, silk flowers, ribbons, and all sorts of things for craft projects.

"When I first poked my head in this room, all I really saw were the books and the couches."

"You were just getting your head around where you were," reminded Ruth. "There will be things that pop up in view that you had never before noticed even when you had looked at it a hundred times. It's kind of like when Christy would read the Bible out loud so that we also could enjoy. A passage she would read multiple times before can give us a different understanding depending on what is currently going on at the moment. It is how the Master speaks with us, reminding us of how much more he has for us in learning, loving, and just plain being."

"Sure are a lot of books on that wall," remarked Dittims as he gazed floor to ceiling.

"Seems to be." Ruth chuckled. "Those are all the books that she has read so far. But in reality, she is not that much of a reader. If you get the chance to go to her daughter's house"—Ruth chuckled with emphasis—"now *that* is a library and of course still growing by leaps and bounds. She reads about a book a week. So I can't imagine how big it will be by the time she gets here."

"Hi, guys." Azer yawned as he stretched while coming into the room. "What are you doing in here?"

"Just keeping quiet so the others could still rest," explained Dittims.

"Wow, what a comforting room, so peaceful." Azer sighed as he settled with the others on one of the couches.

"There has always been something special about this room," said Ruth, "not really sure what it is."

"I checked on food, and it will be a little bit before it is ready," commented Azer.

"Yes," affirmed Ruth. "Seems we had a new chef starting, and the first attempt did not work as expected, so she is backing up and punting as it were. Are the others up and about?"

"Yea, I think Sam is even up."

OUR HOME OF LOVE

"Why don't we start off in here this morning?" asked Dittims. "Then we can change places after we eat if we want to."

"Sounds like a good idea," agreed Ruth. "Azer, would you mind getting everyone?"

"Sure."

Dittims got off the couch and wandered toward the windows facing the front yard. "Who takes care of the house—you know, like the simple everyday things that get done without thinking? I know we can do a lot of things to help, but we don't have hands. I might be able to open a window a little bit, but it would not be much."

"Remember," explained Ruth, "there are a lot of people here that love to help each other, just like we have a new chef today in the kitchen. God's gift to each human is different. Therefore their talents and interest are different, and they all, as well as us, come together to get all things done for his kingdom all the way down to helping keep houses organized for people who have yet to arrive."

"I saw a lot of houses as I first arrived, and this is only one house on our street."

"True, it will take you time to wrap your mind around all of this. This is only one house on one street from one district in one sector off one plateau."

"Wow. Wait," said Dittims as he twirled to face Ruth, "there is more than one plateau."

"All in good time, Dittims," soothed Ruth. "We are a small speck in a very large plan that the Master has for his kingdom."

"Amazing," said Dittims as he walked back to the couch.

"Oh, I love this room," oozed Munchkin as she and the others began entering.

"Yes, Dittims suggested we start here, and I agreed it would be a nice change. We can start here first, and then after we eat, we can move or come back here if we want," explained Ruth.

"Sounds like a good plan to me," said Gypsy as she headed to the window for a good sniff of fresh air flowing in through the windows. "I think I will pull a cushion by this window. It smells so wonderful over here."

As everyone settled on either a cushion on the floor or on one of the couches, they turned their attention to Sam, who had settled more center stage of the floor for all to see.

"To remind Dittims of a few things," said Samantha, "Christy is not my full-time caretaker. I am one of those dual partners like Spot, but I am pretty evenly split between Christy and her mom, and very similar to Muffin that you met down at the community center. We both kind of coshare between the two homes, but since I was there when Christy was younger, I can fill in on some earlier stories, and Muffin will have later stories from Christy's adult years, so we will probably swap places depending on what is going on at the time. I was given as a gift to Christy's mother by CJ when Christy was a teenager. Gypsy, you were still there."

"Yes," said Gypsy. "You were quite adorable tripping on your long ears with your big feet."

"The thrills of being a basset." Sam sighed.

"Christy's mother had longed for a basset for several years," continued Sam. "Christy's father had found a stuffed one at an airport during one of his business trips and brought it to her. She put it on top of the piano so she could see it when she played. Her father was just not ready for a house dog. The dogs in his life had been trained hunters, and he was not yet of the mind-set for a dog as a house pet."

"I was his first nonhunting hunter he had ever had," piped in Spot. "The small dogs around the house, Nellie and Sandra, had been dogs for the kids. Later in his life when he became so fond of CJ's dog Sugar, did he ever think of having a dog that slept on his bed with him, Charlie, also a gift from CJ."

"Along with CJ, Christy's other sister Sarah and her brother Ben all share the same love for dogs. When other dogs met them, those dogs can sense that love this family possessed for four-legged creations," commented Nellie.

"During the earlier times, people were not of the mind-set for dogs to be housemates and best friends," commented Spot. "That came later as they started creating specialty and show breeds."

"Well," continued Sam, "CJ was out on her own and was in the dog-breeding business and had contacts with people who bred bassets. She knew how much her mom had wanted a real basset puppy, so she got her me. It was all very exciting. I had Christy's mom to love on me, plus Christy and her brother. And because I was a puppy, well, most everyone loves a puppy."

Knowing nods went around the room.

"If it only lasted through our growing up," commented Zero. "Some owners just don't understand the long-term commitment that is needed in having a pet."

"Fortunately for all of us," continued Sam, "we belonged to several generations of families who loved us for the long haul. And some of us really got to do fun things as the family grew. You have heard others speak of the Florida trips, but after I came along, they had bought a house of their own, so then it was no trouble to take pets along, and lots of us got to go there. Both of Christy's sisters and her brother had pets, and when they would visit, the pets got to come as well." Sam chuckled. "Sometimes, there seemed to be as many dogs as there were people. Many of my favorite times are from the Florida house. And there were a few not-so-favorite memories as well."

"How about the time you got plastered?" Munchkin laughed.

"I was not plastered—a little tipsy, maybe. It was an accident as well. I was thirsty, and there was a glass on the ground that my caretaker was drinking. I had taken, as we all have," defended Sam as she looked around at everyone, "scraps from people with no concerns. How was I to know this was bad stuff?"

Chuckles flittered around the room.

"For my benefit as I have never heard this story"—Dittims chuckled—"can I get the whole story?"

"Oh, all right," moaned Sam in mock exasperation. "It's one of those stories you never live down, and we all have them."

"But the visual on this one is quite humorous," agreed Gypsy.

"Okay, here's a little background information we are all doing for your benefit, Dittims. The Florida house was in a small town below Tallahassee on the gulf coast. In the summer, it gets really hot, and everyone is always drinking some sort of beverage to keep cool. There were even two large water bowls for us four-legged creatures. As customary for each house and family, there were lots of chairs on the front lawns to sit in and visit with neighbors or to just sit and enjoy the view. Since the house was on a bay, there were no waves, but the water and trees were very peaceful to enjoy. This one day, the families on both sides of Christy's family came over to visit, and they were all talking and enjoying themselves. Some people had wire stands that would hold your beverage to keep if off the ground so that ants would not get in it, but Christy's parents did not have any of these, so they just placed their glasses on ground. My water bowl was empty, and I was thirsty, so I went to see if she would refill my bowl. They were so busy chatting they didn't notice me, so I thought I was just drink some of her water. Only it wasn't water. I knew it tasted funny, but she was drinking it, so I knew it would not hurt me, and it was cold because there was ice in it. And I drank about half the glass before someone noticed and yanked it from me. I thought they were going to be real mad since they were moving so fast, but they just laughed about it. A short time later, I didn't feel so well. It was like I was a puppy again, being dizzy and tripping on my ears and such."

"You were drunk!" teased Munchkin. And several members were rolling in laughter on their cushions.

"You know we love you, Sam," comforted Ruth. "It's just a funny thing that happened."

"I know, and everyone knows I didn't do it on purpose."

"But"—Munchkin sighed—"that's what makes it so adorably funny.

"Were there other stories involving alcohol?" asked Dittims jokingly.

"Not involving me, but there was the time when Christy was a teenager and their parents decided to have a New Year's Eve party in the garage."

"The garage," asked Dittims shockingly, "a dirty old smelly garage, and cold at that time of year?"

"Well," explained Sam, "they had just built a nice two-car garage at the Florida house and decided to have a dedication party there as a kind of housewarming idea for the holiday."

OUR HOME OF LOVE

"Sounds like just an excuse to me," commented Munchkin, "to have a party and partake in the bubbly."

"Yea, that was pretty much it," agreed Sam, "but with lots of tasty morsels that I got to have because the more bubbly they drank, the cuter I got, and the more tasty bits I received. It was fabulous. That's when Christy decided to try the bubbly herself, encouraged in teasing by her brother Ben, who by that time was in college and more understanding of how the world worked."

"Oh, not good," moaned Dittims.

"Yes and no, depends on how you look at it," continued Sam. "When Christy's father realized what she was doing, he was not happy with her. But something her brother said made him stop and take notice a bit, but still he remained unhappy and concerned."

"I had forgotten about this story," said Ruth. "What was it that Ben said, 'something about testing at home'?"

"Ben made a matter-of-fact statement to their dad," reminded Sam, "asking him would he rather her try it at home, where he could supervise or in a bar when she headed off to college."

"Wow," said Dittims, "that's bold, but I guess there is some truth there. Did she do a lot of tasting of alcohol when young? I do not ever recall her even having it around the house."

"I don't think so that I ever saw," commented Sam.

"As an adult, I never knew of her drinking much alcohol other than an occasional glass of wine with friends," said Ruth. "Maybe that incident was all she needed to let her know that was something she didn't enjoy."

"Overconsumption can be a dangerous thing," added Sandra. "I remember some boat trips that could have turned bad quickly if the wrong person had been the one to be not thinking properly."

"Indeed," continued Sam, "there were quite a few incidents that I shake my head on in wonder that no one was hurt. There was one in particular that was on the scary side, but I did not understand the fear until everyone got home and I listened to Ben talking about it. Christy, Ben, and their father had gone fishing out in the gulf. And again, I was not there, but the story stuck with me due to how

Christy and her brother told the story to their other sister who had also been down for the weekend.

"As Gypsy has stated, boat types changed from flat-bottomed cabin boats, which are great for rivers, to V-shaped hull boats, that could tolerate the moderately rough gulf waves if needed. And this boat could be seen off in the distance due to its striking blue color.

"They would go out to certain buoys and fish for small baitfish and then go trolling for the bigger fish. This one day, fishing had been real good, and they forgot to keep an eye on the fuel. When they realized this could be an issue, they were well out of sight of land, so they turned for home hoping they would make it. The boat was equipped with a radio, so they called in to the marina where they kept the boat and let them know the situation. They said they would send someone out if they ran out. Well, they did run out, but Christy's father had been a sailor and knew a lot about boats. He noticed that the nice breeze they had been feeling all day was actually blowing toward home, so he raised the canopy covering the captain's chairs into the wind, and that acted like a sail and moved them toward home. Pretty soon, they were in sight of land and could see a boat heading our way. It was one of the mechanics from the marina bringing them fuel. He came on board and brought two cans of gas to get them home. Ben grabbed Christy and pulled them both to the very front of the boat on top of the bow. He kept watching the mechanic and Christy's father pour gas in the tank. When finished, both boats headed back into port."

"Oh, that's good," said Dittims.

"They got home with plenty of daylight to clean all the fish they had caught. I went out for a while to see the various fish but got in the way, so I came on back inside. The dock did have lights at the cleaning station, but first dark is known as mosquito heaven, so they wanted to get finished before dusk. Later that evening, I heard Ben talking about how scared he had been watching the two men pour fuel into the tanks. Both men had cigarettes dangling from their mouths, and the gulf was a little rough, causing the boat to rock, and if either man had slip or dropped their cigarette, it could have been real bad. Gas fumes and cigarettes are never a good mix."

"I think I have said it before that I don't understand why you would deliberately breathe in poisonous air. I just do not get it," said Gypsy.

"Yea, television marketing can make a lot of different things popular that should never be popular," commented Sandra.

Chapter 16

> A dog is the only being on earth that
> loves you more than he loves himself.

"What were some of the other stories you remember from the Florida house, Sam?" asked Dittims.

"The walks were the best. We would walk down the beach in front of the houses or drive down to the point where the road ended in a parking lot. That area was real shallow and flat, so you could walk out far at low tide and explore things that would get washed up at high tide. And the horseshoe crabs were everywhere, such a funny-looking creature. You didn't get too many shelled creatures as it was an inlet of the gulf, but it was a great place to go gigging for flounder. Christy had several local friends that taught her all about various fishing and crabbing tricks for the area. I remember her coming home with two flounder during one night's fun with friends. Her mother was very excited. It is such an ugly fish to evidently taste so good."

After a thoughtful pause, Sam continued on. "I also liked the walks Christy, her father, and I would take in the woods across the street from the house. There was a dirt road that led down to the bay on the other side of the point. It was a wonderful stretch of woods and great place for quail and deer. I remember when I was young, 'the call of the wild' got me."

Laughter filled the room. "No offense, Sam, but I can't imagine you having any kind of energy to be classified as wild," teased Ruth.

"Well, I was young and a hunting breed. Christy and I had decided to go for a stroll down the dirt road through the woods. There evidently were hunters in the area as we heard gun fire, so we turned to go home. As we turned to head home, this rabbit skittered through the brush and jumped right out in front of us on the dirt road. It looked at me for a split second, then took off, and I was right behind it. I almost had it once too. I lost track of it in the palmetto plants after a bit and turned to head back toward Christy as she was calling for me. Just as I turned to go in that direction, a deer ran right in front of me, and chasing him were two beagles, Sampson and Daisy. They hollered at me to follow them, so I did, for days," moaned Sam. "Well, really just through the night until early the next morning. Christy had been dreadfully concerned for me, but her dad told her not to worry that I knew my way home. And he was right, and I was so glad to have a home to go to. When I got there, Christy was so glad to see me. But I went straight to the water bowl, emptied it, and then crashed under the dinner table on the cool tile and slept all day and that night. It was fun, but that is way more work than I ever want to do again."

Giggles of understanding filled the room. "That's the Samantha that I know," teased Ruth.

"I do remember fun times lying on the beach with Christy where we would howl together. She usually went to the beach with towel and book and would call me over to be with her. When we got settled, she would call my name in a soft high-pitched baying manner, and I would answer by calling her name in my deep soft baying manner. Although I know she could not understand my language, she just thought I was baying with her. But it was a wonderful time of being together. I remember when she brought her boyfriend from college down, and they went down to the beach. I followed them down, and when I got close, I was going to do our baying game that we loved to do. So I let out with my deep bay, and that guy moved so fast you would have thought I was an attack dog. Christy saw me coming and knew what I was going to do, so I guess she just wanted to see what he would do. He moved very fast."

Laughter filled the room.

"Too bad you didn't just chase him away like the German shepherd. Could have saved a lot of problems later," commented Gypsy.

"You don't really know that," replied Ruth. "You don't know what other problems could have happened in other situations. God always has a plan."

"I know, but we all just wanted to take care of her like she took care of us," mused Sam, remembering all the fun they had while they were together.

"You know the reason for all the art supplies here in the library was that she studied art in high school and in college," continued Sam. "She created a painting of me once. It was quite cool. I had on an old fishing hat with fishing barbs hanging off it. I had never seen that hat but the idea came from a photo she had of me in the front yard down at the beach house."

"Oh, now that's cool," exclaimed Dittims. "Whatever happened to it?"

"I don't know. Shortly after it was completed, she headed off to college."

"What about the statue she made while in college that you told us about once?" asked Zero.

"Oh, I forgot about that. It was a Christmas gift for her mom. She really did like it too. Christy got her artiness from her mom as she was always doing some sort of needlework. From the comments I heard when others were talking about her mom's work showed she had a real knack for that kind of stuff."

"I bet you missed Christy when she left for school," said Dittims.

"I did miss my playmate, but Christy's mom was my true caretaker. She was quiet and read a lot while watching TV, which was okay with me. By that time, I was ready to sleep…all the time."

Chuckles murmured through the room.

"Did you still go on Florida trips?"

OUR HOME OF LOVE

"Oh yes, almost every weekend. But it was funny, since I didn't have a lap to be in on the trip, Christy's mom made me some canvas booties to wear. She was concerned my nails would puncture the seats. They felt kind of weird, but, whatever, I wore them."

"Did Christy come home much from school?" inquired Sandra. "She was such a quiet thing when I knew her and such a homebody."

"Well, the school was in the northern part of the state, so it was several hours' drive. Christy's father bought her a car, though, so that she could come when she wanted to. Evidently, colleges have mascots, and I knew Christy's college choice was right for her since theirs was a dog, a bulldog I believe. She would come home from school yelling, 'Go, Dogs,' although when she wrote it on paper, it was a different kind of spelling. She spelled it *Dawg*. Weird but she was happy, so that's all that mattered at that point. She did come home to complete her last few classes at the local college so that she could plan her wedding. It was nice having her home."

"Was it a nice wedding?" asked Dittims.

"Well, I don't really know. A week before the wedding, I got real sick and came here. I guess it was a sad time, especially with everything that was going on."

"Yes," commented Gypsy. "She took it real hard. Y'all had gotten close again like when you were young."

"Wait a minute," inquired Dittims, "how do you know how hard it was for Christy?"

"We all stay in touch with how things are going with Christy," explained Ruth. "She took care of all of us, and we, in turn, monitor how she is doing through the Master. He keeps us informed, and there is a possible way, if the need is strong enough, for a brief interlude to nuzzle and say hi. Not that she would recognize it as us, but we would know."

"What?" exclaimed Dittims. "How is that possible?"

"With the Master," Ruth gently whispered, "all things are possible. He sends his messengers down to help as the need arises, and it has been known that he will let one of the major canines go. But it is for extreme cases and very brief visits."

"Oh, wow," exhaled Dittims, "have any of y'all ever been?"

"No. Fortunately, Christy has not had an extreme need. It got close once, though," pondered Ruth. After a moment, she continued, "Samantha, have you got more to share for now, or are we ready for a short break? I saw the chef nod that food was ready."

"I think I am good for now. Like the others, I have more that can be shared at a later time."

"That's true," said Ruth. "After eating, why don't we take a stroll by the pond? I heard they were putting in a new fountain head in the pond fountain. A short time ago, some over zealous workers tried to adjust the fountain for a higher stream than it was capable of. In doing so, they broke the main feeder line and it has not been working properly since."

"That's a good call," informed Zero. "I saw the gardener bringing over those bird's nest evergreens that were we going to add as well. I want to see how it looks."

"I saw them earlier, and they look real nice," said Ruth as they were heading toward the kitchen. "But I still think something is not quite right. Let me know what you think. Maybe you will have a good idea once you review it."

"Sure, we can go by there first before going down to the pond."

"Sounds like a plan."

After the meal, they all decided to review the placement of the evergreens where Trip had tried to be so helpful.

"I see what you mean," said Sandra, "but I am wondering how much that bush will grow. If you add anything more, will it get crowded?"

"Those evergreens don't get very big or grow very fast," commented Zero. "What we could do is plant some small border plants that can adapt with it as it grows."

"That's a good idea. See," said Ruth, "that's why I wanted you to review it. You have spent more time at the community garden than I have, and you have a better eye for things like that than I do."

"I do like the way that plant fills in the indention that was there," commented Gypsy. "It gives that slight slope some character of its own."

"This type of greenery may make a nice accent piece for the back side to some of the raised gardens, especially the one that has the latticed backdrop," mentioned Ruth. "I have been trying to think of something for those to make them less hard, if that is the right word. Let's go over to that bed, and let me show you what I am talking about."

As they came around from the front of the house to where the raised bed in question was located, Ruth stopped for a moment to review the area.

"Yes, I think evergreens may be a nice addition. This is the only bed that is square. It does have the tiers for character, but all showmanship of the bed is in one direction. If we add evergreens, and there are several other types to choose from, we can give the entire bed a new look."

"What are you seeing in your head, Ruth?" asked Zero.

"Well," she said as she walked around the bed, "we know the back of the bed is not really unusable due to the lattice backdrop for the Confederate Jasmin. But if we put some of the midsized evergreen shrubs like the mop cypress, that would provide a low-maintenance and character-building look to this bed."

"Thought you didn't know much about gardening," teased Zero.

"I don't really. My favorite section in the maze has several types of evergreens, so I have learned a little bit about those."

"What about something on either side toward the last tier?" added Sandra. "Maybe something that blooms."

"Or a boxwood that you can cut into a fancy or quirky shape," said Nellie.

"All of those are good suggestions. Zero, could you get with James the next time you go down to the community center and see when he is available to speak us. He always has good ideas and is aware of new things being created from the botanist on board at the center."

"Consider it done. Maybe Dittims and I will plan a walk there so I can show him around that part of the complex."

"Good, keep me posted to make sure I am available when he is available. Let's go down and see if they have completed the fountain. There is not much breeze today, but it still feels good being outside."

Chapter 17

⁂

> If they love, they are aware. If they
> are aware, they have a soul.
> —A. D. Williams

"This is actually a natural time for a break," explained Nellie as they settled down on the benches at the pond, "because at this point in Christy's life, she was taking a break from having a pet."

"Well, it kind of wasn't her choice," commented Gypsy. "She was in college in a dorm, and they don't allow dogs."

"What about Dagu?" chimed in Sam. "She didn't have him but two months, but it was an interesting two months of a summer semester with lots of hiding and sneaking around at all hours."

"Dittims, you met Dagu down at the community center. He goes by Jetson from his final family. Christy had a hall mate in the dorm whose family had recently lost their long-time pet, and she gave him to them when she realized she was going to get herself and Dagu in trouble if she didn't do something right and quickly."

"I did meet him," said Dittims, "but I am not aware of the story."

"Okay," explained Sam, "as we all know, Christy loves dogs and knew she could not have one in the dorm, so she volunteered down at the local shelter so she could be around dogs and other animals.

Someone had dropped off a box of six puppies at the door before they even opened one Saturday, and they melted Christy's heart."

"It was the summer semester with very few people in the dorms, and she did not think through to reality and took one of the puppies to be with her at the dorm. She lived on the fifth floor but was able to housebreak Dagu in about three weeks. He was really a smart puppy or just had a strong sense about what he needed to do. The ladies that kept the dorm clean knew of this, of course, but because they had made friends with Christy, they looked the other way as much as they could. She always cleaned up anywhere Dagu had done his business, so no one really knew there was a dog living in the dorm."

"Dagu," pondered Dittims, "that's kind of an odd name."

"Well, you know how quirky Christy was. After all, your nickname is Dittims," teased Sam. They all chuckled knowing Christy was indeed quirky at times.

"Anyway, she was at university, with a dog, so she played around with the letters, and that is what she came up with by placing the letters backward and adding *D* for dog and came up with Dagu. And fortunately for Christy and Dagu, she had made good friends with the girl across the hall, and their family was looking for a puppy. So one weekend, Dagu went to live with them. When the semester was complete, Christy got to go visit the family and Dagu, I mean Jetson, for the weekend, and, of course, Jetson met her with lots of kisses."

"Did she continue to work at the shelter?" asked Dittims.

"No, she tends to stay away from them even now. She knows she would probably bring them all home if she could. She doesn't even like watching the commercials on TV about abused animals and abandoned pets, too hard for her to watch."

"Big heart." Ruth sighed.

"Hey, Nellie," reminded Sam, "remember the time you were with the Master checking in on Christy about the grocery store incident?"

"Oh yea, I forgot about that. That was when you were there, Zero. Right after Christy had given birth to her first child."

"Yea," said Zero, "that guy was not happy with the note she left on his car. He called the house before Christy even got home from the store and yelled at her husband. I could hear it through the phone. But surprisingly, he took up for her and told him that if she had the guts to write him a note and leave her phone number on it, then it must be true and that she could report him to the police for abuse."

"What in the world did that guy do?" asked Dittims.

"In the middle of summer in the south," Zero continued, "it gets really hot really fast inside a car with the windows up, and some caretakers are careless by leaving their pets in the cars while they run into the store. They think they are just going in for a few minutes and have no clue how hot it can get in a matter of minutes inside a closed-up automobile. I have seen people leave their young children in that same situation. It's so very dangerous.

"Anyway, this guy had left his dog in the car and went in the store. Christy pulled in right after him and saw all the windows up and knew it was already getting hot. She ran in and picked up the few items she needed, and still the owner had not returned, so she wrote a strong note and put it on his windshield with her phone number because she wanted him to know just how serious this was, but he called before she got home and didn't get a chance to speak with him herself."

"You know," remembered Gypsy, "when Christy was young, her neighbors lost two dogs one summer for that very reason. Their son, who was pretty young at the time, had forgotten to let them out of the car when they got to their lake house. By the time the family realized the dogs were missing, it was too late."

"Oh, that is so sad."

"Yea," continued Gypsy, "the older dog, Buster, was a good friend of mine. We were about the same age. He lives over in Area 63."

"Okay, enough sadness. We are in a happy place," roused Zero. "Happy story time, Sam, tell about your car rides."

"Oh, those were so fun, especially going to the Florida house. Once Christy got old enough to drive, she took me everywhere, and I always got the window down so I could lean out. My ears would be flying in the wind. It was great."

"Even when going fast," asked Dittims.

OUR HOME OF LOVE

"Oh no," explained Sam. "If we were on the highway, Christy would not allow the window to be open. She didn't want me to get hurt from strong wind, but the slower speeds were okay. I remember the trips going to Florida where we went down the back roads that did not have a lot of traffic on them. There was this one road Christy nicknamed The Long Lonesome. It was an eleven-mile stretch through timberland that covered the last bit of Georgia going into the first edge of Florida. Christy would slow down and let me poke my head out. Some of the areas had been harvested and replanted, and some areas were still full of tall swaying pine trees.

"One time, when the family was coming home after dusk, Christy's father hit some sort of small wild animal that ran across the road in front of the car. He stopped to see if he could see it and check on the damage to the car, but it ran into the woods, and the car seemed okay other than slight damage to the headlight. They continued on with one light shining to the side of the road until they got to the next town located on the other side of the Long Lonesome. He stopped at a gas station to get a better view of the damage and had the gas station attendant look at it, too, to see if he could repair the headlight. The attendant pulled out hair from around the headlight and told her father he had hit a bear. Her father was shocked thinking he had hit a wild pig as there were quite a few in that area."

"Oh wow, that could have been so dangerous if the bear had come after him. A hurt animal is even more dangerous that it is normally, and a bear, oh my," said Dittims.

"Plus," reminded Ruth, "if that bear was small enough for her father to think it was a pig, it was probably a baby, meaning there was probably a mama bear close by. It never ceases to amaze me how, in hindsight, we are always protected. The Master can take a bad situation and somehow show the good side of it. You just have to know how to look for the signs."

"Hello, everyone, how are you?" greeted a sable and white likeness to Samantha.

"Muffin, how are you?" greeted Ruth.

"Doing well. I am headed up to Jones's farm. Trip was telling me that Sarah had some really nice spices in the small garden behind the barn. I was going to see if she had any dill. Grace is ready to get those cucumbers she is growing into pickle spices and get them canned."

"Dittims, you remember Grace from the watermelon cutting? She is Christy's mom," said Ruth.

"Yes, I do. Christy really favors her. Although I think I was more taken by CJ. I almost thought I was looking at Christy."

"Yes, the resemblance is strong in that family," said Muffin, "with CJ, Ben, and Christy really favoring their mom. Sarah does as well but not quite as strong. And that looked got passed down to Christy's youngest from what I understand. And remarkably, his son is a mini me of him carrying on that same family resemblance. It's funny how that works because Christy's mom did not have a strong resemblance to either of her parents. It was just a good blend."

"Well, good luck on finding the spices you need. Tell Trip I said hey," said Sandra. "And if you have time, come by for some story time," said Ruth.

"I will do that. Take care, and I will try to get by later."

"Such a friendly sort," commented Dittims.

"Yes, she always has been," agreed Ruth.

The group grew quiet in their own thoughts for a time, being relaxed and enjoying the warmth of the air as they watched the small fish swim among the lily pads. The fountain was still not working, but boxes of equipment were lying around with the promise of the work coming soon. A slight breeze filtered through the air, bringing a mix of various flower fragrances and the occasional whiff of freshly baked bread from somewhere. A slight rumble from the group brought on soft giggles when all realized Sam was fast asleep, totally at peace with everything. The others just stretched and sighed, fully enjoying the moment in quiet harmony. Ruth spied Spot as he was coming down to join them. He had a purplish mark on one side of his muzzle. "What have you been sampling there, Spot?" she teased.

"Some sort of fruit pie chef is experimenting with. It has raspberries and blackberries and a superflaky crust. It was so good. Have I still got it on my face somewhere?"

OUR HOME OF LOVE

"Yep, right side of your muzzle."

"That bakeoff that is coming," reminded Zero, "is really going to be something. I was over at Rusty's a few days ago, and his Christy was making something with veggies folded in this thin-layered pastry. It smelled delightful."

"She didn't let you taste it?" asked Sam, rousing at the mention of food.

"Ah, sleeping beauty is back with us," teased Zero. "No, I left before it was done."

"Well, lunch is almost done," mentioned Spot, "with fresh peas and potatoes from the garden, sliced cucumbers, and tomatoes in a light vinegar drizzle for those of us who like the sharp sour tastes, the usual raw-broccoli-and-carrot mixture and yummy cheese bread chunks."

"And pie," reminded Ruth.

"Yes"—Spot sighed, nodding—"very berry pie. Superyummy. Shall we head in?"

As they turned to head up to the house, a loud *snap, crash* caught their attention from up the hill. Sarah Jones, Trip, and Muffin were looking sadly at their cart as a wheel had cracked and fallen off, spilling some of their foods onto the road.

"You guys okay? Do you need any help?" called Ruth.

"No one is hurt, but I think the cart is done for," called back Muffin. She turned to Trip and told him to run go get help. "We will be okay. Trip is heading back to get Bill."

"Okay, you are welcome to join us for lunch if you want," called Spot.

"Thank you," said Sarah, "but we will just wait here for the cavalry. We will catch you next time."

"Okay." And they continued on to the house.

Once inside, the smells from the kitchen filled the hall. "Oh, the smells of freshly baked bread," commented Gracie as they entered into their room.

"You didn't get to be around long for tidbit morsels from Christy, did you?" asked Ruth of Gracie.

"No, I got sick very young. I only got about eight weeks with her before coming here, but that was enough to know I was loved."

"I did not realize that," said Dittims, looking at her, then over at Azer. "It's okay. I was from the litter before you, same parents, just a different birthday."

"I met your brother once," remembered Dittims. "I know I was young, but he was huge. I think he topped out close to two hundred pounds," exclaimed Dittims.

"Yes, he was the biggest of our litter. I heard stories that he devoured a wedding cake about two hours before the wedding."

"No way"—gasped Spot—"a whole wedding cake?"

"Pretty much," continued Gracie. "From what I understand, his caretaker was a wedding planner. She took her eyes off him long enough for him to take a huge bite right out of the second tier, causing the entire cake to fall to the floor. They even had pictures."

"I bet those people we upset." Ruth gasped.

"Surprisingly, they were not, at least not from what I heard. I am sure that were not happy. But they were breeders as well, so they know what can happen if you take your eyes off of us with temptations like right at eye level."

"That's probably true," said Ruth. "I guess when tables are right at your height, special precautions need to be made."

"I heard Christy comment one time," said Dittims, "that when she had gotten used to our size, she would periodically forget just how big we were."

"Azer, you did not make it to adulthood either, did you?" asked Sandra.

"No, I was kind of a weak puppy. Christy picked Dittims because of his coloring, solid white with the one black spot. No one had picked me, and Christy's soft heart felt sorry for me, so she took me as well."

"It didn't surprise me a bit either," said Ruth. "I was getting on in age and Christy didn't want a puppy bothering me where I was not able to tolerate it, but she also thought company might be good for me. So she decided to go ahead and get Gracie. Then she was hooked on the Dane breed. When she lost Gracie and found out they were having another litter, she asked to have one."

"Ah, foods here," said Munchkin, licking her lips.

Various bowls were placed around, and talking ceased momentarily as they gave thanks for their meal.

Chapter 18

> The difference between humans and
> dogs is dogs don't fake love.

"Since we are somewhat on a break from storytelling," assessed Ruth, "this afternoon may be a good time for Dittims to revisit the plateau. He and I had a conversation about it, and maybe it's a good time for a little more education of how things flow."

"That would be perfect for Azer and me," pipped up Gracie, "as we have been asked to bring over some flats of flowers from garden center to one of the arbors that they are replanting."

"Okay. Why don't Dittims and I meet you there in a couple of hours? That will give me enough time to run my errands."

"Do you guys need any help?" asked Dittims. "I saw how Lakota and Skeebo were pulling a small cart of supplies when I first arrived. So I understand how to help with pulling."

"Sure. Extra help is always nice," affirmed Azer.

"Then I and anyone else that wants to go will meet you there in a couple of hours," said Ruth as the giant dogs headed out for the arbor redesign.

When the three arrived at the garden center, they were met by one of the garden specialist who was filling a cart with the supplies they needed for the arbor redesign.

"Hey guys," he said, placing a tray of soft yellow star-shaped flowers on a flat cart. "I see you brought some extra help."

"Yes, this is our brother Junior," introduced Azer. "We all call him Dittims."

"Well, hello, Dittims," he said as he patted him on the back. "Help from you big guys is always appreciated."

"Oh, these are pretty and smell nice too," said Gracie as she was investigating the cart.

"Those are a new variety of clematis developed by one of our botanist. She calls it Summer Breeze. We are going to show case them with arbor redesign."

"Are you going with us to do the planting?" asked Dittims.

"No, a team is already there, clearing out and rearranging. You are a little early, but I am almost finished loading up what they will need to complete the design. They have already taken over the heavier equipment and supplies."

As he went back inside to gather the remaining supplies, Dittims turned to Gracie and remarked, "It's still so fascinating to me how we can work together with each other. Like the cooks helping us out at the house and us helping here with our abilities and everyone working together as a team."

"That was the original plan. Everything just got sidetracked through trickery, and everything fell from there," said Gracie.

"So profoundly sad." Dittims sighed.

"Okay, guys," said the gardener, placing a bag of plant food on the back of the cart. "That should be everything they need. Let's get your harnesses set, and you will be good to go. Thanks for helping out with this."

"Glad to be of help," assured Dittims.

"Okay, so now that we have the flowers," asked Dittims as they were heading toward the plateau, "what is the other purpose or knowledge that Ruth wants me to understand concerning the plateau?"

"Well, I think she is hoping for a homecoming."

"Homecoming?" queried Dittims.

"Be patient as fascinating wonders get revealed to you. If we threw them at you all at once, and in reality we couldn't, you would be overwhelmed. Just relax and take it all in as it comes to you."

"I am assuming you know which arbor we are going to?" asked Azer of Gracie.

"Yes, but from what I understand, it is a large redesign, and we should be able to easily tell which arbor is being worked on."

As they rounded the last curve, they spotted the plateau, and a team of people were digging up plants around one of the shorter arbors on the far side of the plateau.

"Hi," greeted Gracie as the canine team walked up to the gardening team. "We have your flowers and supplies for this redesign."

"Thanks, Gracie. Who are you helpers today?"

"Both are my brothers. Azer is the gray merle, and Dittims is the white. Guys, this is Jay. Jay is also somewhat attached to our love team. He is Christy's grandfather on her mom's side."

"Grace's dad?" inquired Dittims.

"Yes, you met her?" asked Jay.

"Yes, at Districts 51's community center. It was a seed-spitting contest."

Jay chuckled. "Yes, if watermelon is available, she will be there especially if in one of her kids districts."

"Jay had the farm that Nellie came from, and all the stories you heard about the farm were his farm," explained Gracie.

Dittims thought a moment, then made a connection. "They called you Buck."

"Yes, they did. It was my nickname."

"Dittims is my nickname, but Junior is my real name."

"Well, it's great to meet you and Azer both. Let's get you unhooked from these harnesses, and you can go about your day."

As harnesses were unhooked, the three siblings headed over to the fountain to sit and admire the plateau and its surrounding beauty. The mist from the fountain would periodically waft over them in a refreshing wave as the breeze glided around the plateau. Dittims was puzzling again for the reason of the different sectors when a tiny sweet voice caught his attention. He looked in the direction of the voice and saw the Master walking hand in hand with a small child, and Dittims stood to watch them go into Sector 20.

"There are small children here?" Dittims asked in shock.

"New arrival," said Gracie tenderly.

"But she is a small child."

"Think about it, Dittims. How long was I with Christy? And how long for Azer?"

"But that is a person."

"Doesn't matter," affirmed Azer. "We all have a set time for being according to the Master's plan. And those plans have a specific purpose regardless of how short or long."

"There is just so much to learn."

A soft chuckle came from behind him as Ruth walked up to the group.

"Don't let the new information you will learn almost every day overwhelm you. God has a purpose for everything, even you being here, and that's not just to pull carts," she chuckled.

"Everything," she stressed and repeated, "everything is done for love, his love. And we are to fine-tune our thoughts to be like his so that we all work together for his kingdom."

"But not in a week." Azer nudged to help Dittims relax.

"I just don't want to mess up."

"Okay, let's talk about that. This morning, what happened to our breakfast?"

"Well, it was a new recipe that did not work, so she remade breakfast."

"Exactly," affirmed Ruth. "So did she mess up?"

"Of course not, she is just learning."

"And there you have it. We are *all* just learning."

"Okay, okay," said Dittims. "I get it, or I am getting it. Some of us are a little slower than others."

"It's not that you are slower, Dittims," reminded Gracie. "It's that you are newer. One day, you will be a teacher for those newer than you."

"I don't know about all that," he said as the others chuckled with him. "So what lesson do I need to learn from here?" Dittims asked.

"The one you just did," answered Ruth.

"Sorry, I am missing it," explained Dittims.

"What did you just witness that at first bothered you?" reminded Ruth.

"Oh. You mean that little girl being here?"

"That little girl coming home," explained Ruth.

Dittims sat there for a minute, then stood and looked over at the bridge beyond the fountain. The mist again was shimmering rainbow colors all around it. Then he looked at Ruth as his eyes misted over. "The bridge"—he paused—"that's the rainbow bridge Christy used to talk about. This is home…and I am home too."

"You are home too."

They all sat in peaceful silence for a while, listening to the fountain as the water moved through its different levels and splashing into the pool.

"Explain to me about these different sectors. Why did I go to Sector 19 and that little girl went to Sector 20?"

"That has to do with age or time as it were," explained Ruth. "You are beginning to understand the time span of our Love Team as it concerns with Christy's life, but that is only one grain of sand in the massive ocean of people who have lived since the beginning when God first created man."

"You mean Adam?"

"He was the first."

"So he lives down one of these sectors?"

"No. The sectors off this plateau represent the time line after Jesus. Each sector represents a century. Christy was born in the 1900s, so her final home is in Sector 19. That little girl is from this current century which is Sector 20."

Dittims scanned the plateau, looking at all of the beautiful gates with each one having its own distinctive flower combinations. He was trying to take in all the new information without his head exploding.

"What is *before*?" he asked. "It seems to have its own plateau."

"It does. That plateau is time before Jesus. And it has gates just like these here. It is much, much larger. This plateau is relatively new in the grand scheme of things and will add new sectors as time goes forward until…the end of time when God's plan is complete and everyone is here."

"Wow. I remember Sasha telling me we could go into the different sectors. I just didn't realize what she was talking about."

"I heard one of the more experience people here say he thought there were even divisions of plateaus," said Gracie, "but I haven't even fully grasped this one yet."

"Well, think about something for a second," explained Ruth. "Genesis tells of the Master creating the heavens and the earth. Heavens is plural. What we have come to understand is that there are three heavens. And the middle heaven has over one billions galaxies similar to the one our earth is in. We are only just getting our heads around just how big his plan is."

"I know I am going to regret asking another question," moaned Dittims, "but what do you mean by three heavens? We are currently in heaven, right?"

"Yes, we are. We are in the third heaven, the Master's heaven. During creation, Genesis talks about an expanse being created, separating the waters from below with the waters from above. This expanse is called sky. That is the first heaven. The second heaven is where all the galaxies are located, including our earth."

"With other galaxies," continued Dittims, "does that mean there is more than one earth?"

"I am not sure what all exists now, but I do know that Revelations tells us that a new earth will be created at the end of time. We just don't really know what the entire Master's plan involves," explained Ruth. "But man will have eternity to figure it all out. Come on, let's head back toward the house," encouraged Ruth to the group.

As they were heading back, Dittims's mind was zooming though the new information.

"Do I dare go in the opposite direction of our discussion by asking if the different divisions within the sectors have a meaning or purpose?"

Snickers rumbled through the group. "I know this one," pipped up Azer. "Those represent the year of the person's birth."

"And the house number?"

"House numbers have multiple meanings," informed Ruth, "and I think you have had enough education for one day. I think an evening meal and a relaxing walk through the maze are in order to finish out this day."

"I think I have more questions now than before." Dittims sighed.

"You will get used to it," assured Azer as he gently nudged his brother.

As they rounded the curve near the house, they could see two people inside the pond where Gypsy, Nellie, and Sandra standing near the edge.

"What's up?" asked Ruth as they came up beside them at pond.

"This new fountain head has lights," explained Gypsy, "so while David is completing the installation, Jessica is updating the plants with some night bloomers."

"Oh, that will be nice," commented Ruth. "I know that Christy loves night blooming fragrances."

"Wait," chimed in Dittims, "I thought there was no more night, that the brightness we see is God's light."

"That is very true," replied David. "But at certain times of the new evening, as it is referred to, the light is dimmed so that we may enjoy the beauty of the heavens. The old form of night with deep darkness allowing evil to roam free is gone."

"The Master still wants us to enjoy all of his creation," reminded Ruth, "and the heavens with all the stars and the planets have always been a curiosity with man. Man is born curious and always wanting to explore. It may be an unexplored place on earth, the depth of the seas, the draw of the heavens, or even the tiniest of creation. And it will continue here with different abilities and a new purpose with amazing fascination."

"Those look nice," said Gypsy as she watched Jessica added some plants with dark-green foliage to one of the pots on a raised platform inside the pond.

"These are Arabian tea jasmine," explained Jessica. "They are exceptional night bloomers which, to me, accentuate the beauty you see in the evening with their light sweet fragrance. I had heard this home was fond of the confederate jasmine vine, and I thought this would be a good addition. In the various pots around the pond, we are adding a variation of the lavender angel trumpet, which is also a night bloomer and has a fragrance that complements the Jasmine."

"Are the lights white or colored?" asked Dittims, remembering the fountains he had seen that had multicolored lights.

"These are actually a soft yellow," explained David, "that will give off a relaxing glow to enhance your evening view of the heavens. It should be ready soon so that you may enjoy this evening."

"That will be a wonderful thing after all of today's learning," said Dittims.

"Yea," agreed Azer, "understanding about the plateaus gives you better perspective on the massiveness in size of this place. It's the beginning of understanding of just how much love God has for all of his creation. But I promise Dittims, once you get your head around that, things begin to make sense, and you will be able to prioritize your thoughts. This then allows you to focus on his plan for you and how you, along with all of us, work toward his ultimate plan. It's all about teamwork."

Chapter 19

> Every dog's life starts as a blank canvas. His destiny is determined by the artist, so paint lovingly.

Again, Dittims woke early as was becoming his nature, so he decided to go enjoy the grounds while the others were still resting. He was relaxing on the gazebo when a gentle voice came from behind.

"Good morning. I see you are an early riser as well."

Dittims froze in place as he stared voiceless at the Master. He bowed his head and spoke gently. "Good morning. I again thank you for allowing me to be here."

"You are welcome. Your gentle ways have earned you many blessings, but I want you to learn as much as you can from everyone here. I want you to realize that even though you don't see it, you have a very strong character. Learn who you are here. Learn what others think of you here and gain the confidence I initially gave you. You will need that assured strength and confidence one day."

"As I am learning and feeling what your original plan was, I don't understand why and how very far your creation has slipped away from its intent. Even now, people do not look to you for guidance. Why?"

OUR HOME OF LOVE

"They have been deceived by the father of lies and turned to the world for answers. That is why there is so much pain. Even once they get here, while they are happy and relieved they are here, they have to learn my truths and my ways before they can be fully engaged. Man and beast alike. It all comes together for the good of everyone and everything. There is much to learn, much to enjoy, and so very many ways to grow. You have just had a tiny taste." He chuckled as he gently hugged Dittims and headed on his way. Dittims did not realize he was still staring off in the distance until Sam came onto the gazebo to get him for breakfast.

"Dittims," she asked cautiously, "are you okay?"

Dittims looked at her, then back again in the direction of where he had gone but could no longer be seen. All Dittims could do was quietly stare at Sam and marvel from what had happened.

"The Master was here, wasn't he?" she asked, and Dittims nodded as he stood to go inside.

"It's okay, big guy. You will get used to him stopping by periodically. He greatly loves all of us."

"His love is almost overpowering. He hugged me," whispered Dittims as they headed back to the house.

"Yep, that's how we all feel—animals and people alike. He has a grand plan that we are all a part of. We just have to wait and learn our strengths, grow from our weaknesses, and fine-tune what we are to do to help facilitate his plan. He will guide us. We just have to be willing."

"But how?"

"You will see. Just be open for the teaching."

The smells of the first meal of the day filled the house. As Sam and Dittims entered the main room, they could smell fresh breads being toasted. Various fruit flavors were floating in the air along with a light sweet smell that Dittims was not familiar with. Everyone in the room noticed the quietness of Dittims but left him alone knowing that sometimes emotions and realizations of where you are can take getting used to.

"Something sure smells good," said Munchkin as she came in the room.

"Yes," agreed Ruth. "It's a wonderful 'fix it like you like it' meal. Grab a bowl, and slide it under each canister of your favorites. Hit the lever on the side, and a premeasured amount will go into your bowl. There is warm grain mush that you can add fruit, honey, or nuts. Or if you prefer the dry grains with cold milk, you can still add the fruit, honey, or nuts. Then there is toast slathered with fresh butter, peanut butter, or cream cheese. And of course, plenty of fresh spring water to drink. Let us give thinks for this feast."

After a warm breakfast, Dittims was feeling much better. He asked Ruth, "What are the plans for today?"

"You in for some more stories?"

"Sure."

"Well, then I guess it is Zero's turn. Dagu was actually the next in line, and we already discussed his time a little bit. He will get with you sometime later for stories he may have. I am sure they were interesting with all the hiding and sneaking around."

"Hey, Zero, don't forget to mention how you got your name," teased Munchkin.

"Well, we need to lay a little groundwork as usual for the time line to get the correct perspective. Christy was through with school and was now married. Her husband did not care as much for dogs as he did cats, and they already had a cat named Tigger. You will see him around and about. The Master has different assignments for our feline friends. Christy's husband agreed to allow her to get a dog as long as he got to pick it out. He had a friend at work who knew my mom's caretaker and about us being born. My mom was a German shepherd cross, and my dad was a mixed midsized breed that lived down the street. I was the runt of the litter, and therefore, Christy's husband thought I would be small, so he chose me. Now according to people who like small dogs like Nellie and Sandra there, I am considered a medium-sized dog, but compared to Dittims and his siblings, I am a small dog." Laughter filled the room as they saw the vast difference when Zero walked up to Dittims.

"In this manner, this is how Christy sizes up dogs. I was on the small size of medium, about thirty-five pounds. For instance, Ruth and Munchkin are what she considered on the large size of medium at about fifty-five to sixty pounds. Samson was also on the upper size of that range. She has had three lab types like y'all, four counting her current pet Mimi, which has black lab bloodlines mixed with coon hound and is also on the higher end of that range at seventy-five pounds."

"Yes," chimed in Munchkin, "I have heard her say she doesn't care as much for the smaller breeds, but as she is getting older, she is leaning back to that size as they are easier to wash and care for. She was hoping Mimi was going to be on the small side of medium because her feet were small, which can usually be a good way to gage for adult size. It just didn't pan out that way for Christy. Mimi's feet are still relatively small but long. She can roll those toes around and hold onto things like they are hands. She will be an asset for you guys once she is here for the ball teams."

The guys chuckled as they looked at their paws for reference.

"But size is not the only consideration when Christy is choosing a friend. Energy level is of importance as well. Like Sandra for instance, she has a lot more energy than I do," reminded Gracie.

"I find it interesting with you guys," commented Ruth, "your breed is a cross of a bull mastiff with a greyhound, and there is nothing slow about a greyhound."

"Yea, we do like running but for short periods," added Dittims. "For me, about four times around the bush playing cup toss and I would be done."

"Maybe that was the draw for our size," continued Zero. "Most all of us this size still like playing like a kid even fully grown. Christy loved playing Frisbee with me. We are also big enough to offer some protection if needed but still small enough for good cuddling."

"As far as protection goes, I believe Mimi is the most intense of all of us," said Ruth. "Where we were protective of the home as well as Christy, Mimi sees a difference between home and Christy when it comes to protection. Her guard is much higher when Christy is home."

"That is because she was a rescue dog," continued Zero. "I have talked a lot with Jake, as he is also a rescued dog. Rescue dogs are more grateful to the person than the place of rescue providing they are rescued to a good loving environment."

"And I was sort of a rescue as well," affirmed Gypsy, "but this is a special family with lots of love to share around."

"Being a part of any of Christy's family members would be a blessing. For instance, Muffin started with Christy's mom and then went to live with Christy's sister Sarah for a short time before going on to Christy's home," added Ruth.

"Yea, she almost went to Ben's house, but he already had two bassets of his own," added Sam.

"I bounced around the family as well," said Munchkin.

"Well," continued Zero, "as you can see, Dittims, we all have stories and can easily be distracted chasing memories in many directions. It's kind of what makes this Love Team unique."

"I know," agreed Dittims. "There were several times I had memories come to mind, but I remained quiet as I want to absorb all that I am learning first."

"So back to my beginning," picked up Zero, "when Christy first saw me, she could not get over the size of my ears or lack of ears. Since I was the runt of my litter, like Sandra was of hers, I was slow to develop. My tail was very short, and my ears were not much more than tiny flaps. So she named me Zero for no ears and tail." Giggles and chuckles filled the room.

"What does *runt* really mean? I have heard that a lot when starting with the family where I was born," asked Dittims.

"Well, it usually means the smallest one or the last one of the litter," Zero explained.

"The last one is usually smaller but not always," explained Ruth.

"By the time I was three months old," continued Zero, "my ears and tail were fully formed, and by six months of age, my ears were standing up like shepherd's ears do. Although I am small in stature per German shepherd standards, you can see that my features favor that breed."

"In looking around the room," mused Munchkin, "besides Sam, I think you Danes are the only pure breeds among us."

"And we all came from the same parents. I was first, and Azer and Dittims are from the same litter the following season."

"Interesting the color difference in y'all," commented Zero. "You are white with marble black, and Azer is gray with marbled black, and, Dittims, you are mostly white except for that one spot of black, and you all have the same parents."

"Yes," continued Gracie. "Our parents were Harlequin Danes, white with marbled black spots. The colorations come from the greyhounds, and they have many colors. The mastiff, our other blood line, is tan, which is the normal coloring for most Danes."

"We seem to be a little off course again, Zero." Ruth chuckled. "So why don't you get us back on track one more time?"

"We were talking about my being a runt, so I wanted to give you a good reference of how small I was. My favorite place to ride at first in Christy's car was on the back windshield area, behind the backseats that was less than four inches wide. The weekend after Christy got me, she was visited by her sister CJ. We went for a ride in the country, and CJ rode in the backseat, and I nestled between her on the back windshield—a very small place. To give you another size reference, when I was grown, I could barely fit my front paws there. Anyway, we stopped at the little country outdoor café for lunch that was nestled by a small stream. After walking down to view the stream, my little legs were tuckered out. Christy had a large shoulder bag that she placed a small towel in, and I nestled down in there and slept though lunch and most of the way back home."

"If I remember correctly, you said it was the navy-and-maroon canvas bag. I remember that bag or one very similar to it," chimed in Ruth. "It was filled with craft supplies and not really much room for a puppy."

"Yep, I was very small at that time, only about seven weeks old and about one good handful for Christy."

"That's tiny," said Dittims.

"But I grew fast as all puppies do. John decided I needed to have my own house, so he built a fine doghouse. It really was too big for me, but sometimes, Tigger would come in it with me to nap."

"Cats don't generally get along with us, but since Christy usually had cats and dogs at the same time, we found ways to get along," commented Ruth.

"I remember that Christy and John loved to play Frisbee, and I would watch them until I figured out how to jump up and catch it. At first, I would run away with it but learned that if I brought it back, I would also get to play. We would play like that for hours it seemed."

"That's probably why you are so good on the Frisbee team," said Gypsy.

"Don't know that I am especially good at it. I just enjoy playing," thought Zero, remembering back.

"When I was about eight months old, we moved from South Carolina to Georgia, where John went back to school. Now that was an interesting move. They rented a small trailer to put their few pieces of furniture and belongings in because my doghouse almost filled the back of John's truck. A lot of doghouses for a dog that stayed inside the people house more than in his doghouse."

"Christy was a firm believer that pets were family. And she liked them being inside bonding with the family members," added Ruth.

"I learned the hard way of how much better that was versus letting my wild side dictate my actions. When I was about three years old, my wild side cost me a hole in my side, puncturing a lung."

"Oh my." Dittims gasped. "Did someone hurt you?"

"Not a person but a deer. It was rut season for the deer, and I took off after one, chasing it through the woods. He turned on me and caught me with his antlers. I got hurt bad enough that it took me two days to get home.

"Christy was really worried when she saw the shape I was in when I did get home. She and John were singing in a church cantata on the day I finally got home. My vet was also a choir member, so when Christy called him, he zipped by the house on his way to the church to look at me. He told Christy that it was serious, one lung was collapsed, and from looks of it, I had lost a lot of blood. He told them that if I made it through the night, I may have a chance. He explained how to keep me wrapped up and pinned up to keep me warm and very still. I was exhausted as well as hurt, so all I wanted to do was sleep, anyway. She did not expect me to still be alive when they got home from the presentation, but I was. The following spring, we moved from the country to a small duplex just on the other side of town. It was closer for John's classes and to Christy's job and provided less opportunity for me to get into trouble. This is where we were living when that guy called about the note Christy left on his car."

"A well-deserved note in my opinion," commented Gypsy.

"It wasn't too long after that when Christy had her first child and my duties changed. I now had someone else to protect. My new sleeping place came to be under the baby bed. I wish I had gotten to know that little tyke a little better, but by the time he was walking, John had finished school and found a job in North Carolina. And as a whole, people were having more house pets, but apartment complexes were generally not willing to accept pets. So they were not going to be able to take me along. They found me a home with friends from church, but I got sick shortly afterward and came here to be with y'all. I had had heart issues from birth, and the new family was a little more stressful than being with Christy. I will tease her when I see her that she broke my heart."

"Aww," whined Sandra.

"It broke both of our hearts really," said Zero quietly. "I saw her crying as they drove off."

"Okay, I will end with a funny story, kind of like Nellie's firework story except this was on John instead of me. At that time, Georgia did not allow fireworks other than the small firecrackers and the bottle rockets. John had several bottles set up in the driveway and was shooting off rockets. At one point, he was bent over lighting a rocket when a small garter snake came from the bushes next to the house where John was standing and scooted right between his legs. In his panic over seeing a snake and trying to get away from it, he hit the bottle holding with the rocket that he had just lit and then sidestepped in a hole, twisting his ankle, and fell. As he hit the ground, the rocket took off the fallen bottle, buzzing right by his head, and the snake was nowhere to be seen."

The friends were rolling on their cushions in laughter, but Ruth shuddered. "Snakes."

"I think I can appreciate John's feelings," said Nellie. "A snake and fireworks, neither sounds like fun."

"Does that wind you up for story time, Zero?" asked Ruth. "I think I could use a short break."

"For now I think, I am sure more will pop into mind as we go."

"I need to bow out for a spell," said Skeebo as he stood. "We still have a little more work to do over in Sector 62, and I told Oscar I would help."

"Perfect timing," said Ruth as she stood. "We can get back together later this afternoon. Samson is actually next in line, and he has already been by. He really did not have a lot of stories as he was not there very long. I guess I am next in line after that."

"Hey, Azer," asked Zero as he stood and stretched, "have you seen the new orange and black fish in the creek that runs through the community gardens?"

"Yes, I have. There is one that is huge. Let's go show Dittims."

"We will meet y'all at the gazebo in a little while," said Zero. "I think we are having vegetable stew for lunch, and that needs to be eaten outside by some of us less graceful members. And I will also speak with Jake and James about the possible design change to that raised bed."

"Okay, you guys try to stay dry," Ruth teased as they left knowing full well they would be more in the creek than watching the fish.

"Well, shall we take a leisurely stroll through the maze?" inquired Sam.

"That sounds like a marvelous idea," approved Ruth.

Chapter 20

> Be silly, be energetic, be selfless, be compassionate, be loyal, be doglike.

As the boys neared the community gardens, Zero saw his friend Jake sunning in a large patch of freshly mowed grass.

"Hey, Jake," Zero called.

"Hey guys, what are you doing down this way?"

"Oh, we came to show Dittims the fish," Zero explained. "Have you met Dittims?"

"I saw him heading your way when he first arrived. It's kind of hard not to see someone of your size coming through. But we have not been formally introduced. Hi, name is Jake," he said as he nodded his head.

"Hey," returned Dittims, "good to meet you."

"Jake, have you seen the new giant gold fish?" asked Zero.

Jake laughed. "You are a goofy guy. Those are koi fish. It's a type of ornamental carp called brocaded carp. And yes, I help get them into their new environment. They were overrun in District 89 and Sector 18's community garden. I went with James over there to pull some out and relocated them here."

"You move stuff to other sectors too?" asked Dittims.

The others just looked at him and then at each other.

"Well, yea," said Jake, amazed at the question. "Have you guys not explained the layout of the land here yet?"

"Not really," said Azer. "He has not been here that long and just was shown about all the different plateaus and sectors yesterday."

"When I first got to the gate, I asked Sasha what the difference was in the sectors, and all she said was, 'Time.' And then yesterday, they explained to me about the sectors and different plateaus."

"Well," continued Jake, "let's see what you remember. When you first came, you arrived at our plateau coming down from the mountaintop, but you could see the two plateaus. Correct?"

Dittims nodded, showing he was with Jake so far.

"And you understand each sector off the plateau represent a century of time. Do you understand about districts?"

"Somewhat. Their districts are also divided by one hundred representing each person's birth year in the district. But the house numbering, I was told, is too complicated for now.

"What about the streets?" asked Jake.

"Not sure I know what you mean," said Dittims.

"Let's do this a different way. What street are you own?"

"Ninth Street," replied Dittims.

"Okay, we are all in Sector 19. That is the twentieth century, years 1900 to 1999. You also are in District 51, making your caretaker's birth year of 1951. The street number is Ninth, signifying that your caretaker was born in the ninth month of 1951, which is September. Are you with me so far?"

"Actually, this is all making sense," said Dittims.

"The house numbering system is a little more complicated because the house identification name changes."

"Okay. Why?" asked Dittims.

"Well, it throws you back into timing again. Before the person arrives here and after they arrive."

"You lost me again," said Dittims, shaking his head in confusion.

"Our house is 904-TC4," piped up Azer. "That is Christy's birthdate, ninth month, fourth day. The *T* is the beginning letter of her last name, the *C* is the beginning letter of the first name, and the

4 represents her birth order in the family—in this case, the fourth child."

"Wow, that's detailed and a little complicated," said Dittims.

"Not once you get used to it," assured Azer to his brother. "It all makes sense, creates a defined order, like everything here."

"Then," continued Jake, "once the person has arrived, they are given a gift from God, a new name that only he knows. And a white stone is given to them with their new name on it. It's not the name that anyone else knows them by but God's new name for them."

"Huh?"

"In chapter 4 of the book of Revelations, Apostle John tells us about the different letters that were written to the seven churches. And all of these letters tell of the good things man was doing and also the things that need improving. He says repeatedly, 'To him who overcomes,' to learn from these letters and to apply them to their lives, to come closer to his ways. To the church of Pergamum, he tells of the gift of a white stone with a new name on it that is known only by the person and God. And I think no one uses that name but God."

Dittims did not answer as he was remembering the white stones he had noticed when he first arrived.

"I noticed some white stones at the end of sidewalks when I first arrived," said Dittims. "They had letters on them, but I could not read them."

"That's because it's special between God and the person."

"Sure is a lot of information over the last couple of days, but things are beginning to make sense."

"Before I get too distracted, I was told by Bill Jones to remind you about transferring some spices he had in abundance. And Ruth wanted me to tell James that she would like his help on a garden project. Is he around?"

"No. He is over at the new project in Area 62, but I will let him know. And thanks for the reminder of the spices. The community center of Area 10 wants to expand their spice varieties."

"Now I beginning to understand that we trade things between the areas and sectors, but I am still curious as to why," asked Dittims.

"You need to change the way you see this place," said Zero. "Even though this is a big place, it is all one big home for all of mankind from the beginning, and we share like a family shares," reminded Zero.

"Man was created in his image to fellowship with him," continued Jake. "Earth is a training ground, so to speak, for the real work that will be done here. We, the animal kingdom, were created as helpers and companions and, as a part of the training process, to show man the true nature of God and how all he wants from man are love and fellowship. We all were created out of love to show the beauty of love and all that it can do.

"So when man gets here, he will have the ability to learn from others here regardless of what area, sector, and evidently different plateaus, although I have not gone past ours yet. Still more, I need to learn myself from here. But for man, it's a wonderful advantage to go see old relatives they had never met or grandparents that were born at the end of one century while the grandchildren are born in the next. Plus there are opportunities to go way back in time to meet people that were talked about throughout history. You need to get your head around that even though this is a huge place, it is still one place, and you can go wherever you want to go. It is a huge learning opportunity. It really is an amazing thing to be able to do even for us. They did tell you about the city?"

"A little, I look forward to visiting there sometime."

"I have been here what seems like a long time and still have only seen a small portion of all there is to see," said Jake.

"Speaking of things to go see," reminded Azer, "let's go look at the fish. I will try not to push anyone in."

"Right." Zero laughed as they headed to the creek.

Dittims looked over the bank of the creek, and it was larger than what he thought it would be. Picnic tables were set on both sides with many flowers lining both sides of the bank. He looked upstream to see children playing in the shallow edges, and adults were sitting on large boulders with their feet dangling in the cool waters as it moved along its way. Downstream, just past Dittims and his friends, the creek flowed into a large pool where you could see the fish as they swam in the crystal clear waters before it moved on through the garden area.

"That's a really colorful fish," said Dittims as he wandered over to the large pool. "He is orange, black, and white."

"I like this one over here," said Zero, looking at a mostly white one with a touch of red around his gills.

"Are koi the only type of fish in here?" asked Dittims.

"Yes, for this section of this creek," confirmed Jake.

"The bigger lakes have the fish that you are probably more familiar with," explained Zero.

After reviewing the pool and that section of gardens, Zero reminded the group of the girls probably waiting on them. "Well, I guess we best head back. We told the others we would not be that long."

"Great meeting you, Jake, and thanks for the lesson. Things are beginning to congeal and make sense now."

"It takes time, and time is what we have lots us."

As they slowly walked back toward the house, Azer asked Dittims how he was doing with all of the information he had been drowned with the last couple of days.

"Okay, I guess. It's a lot to assimilate."

"Do you now understand why we wanted you more comfortable with where you were, having us to lean on and such before we started revealing all of this to you?" asked Zero.

"Yea, now that I think of it like that. And I am sure there is always more?"

"We have only just begun, dude. Come on, we will race you to the gazebo."

*****

"I think this is my favorite section of the maze," said Gypsy as they were relaxing under the canopy of a large maple tree. "I love the light as it winks through the leaves of the trees. The gardenias are especially nice today as well."

"Um, hum," was all Sam could mutter in her half-awake state.

"She can sleep anywhere," teased Munchkin.

"Not anywhere," corrected Sam as she rolled over and sat up on her haunches, stretching and yawning to get fully awake.

Munchkin giggled. "I stand corrected, almost anywhere."

"I heard the chefs talking about the baking event that is coming soon," said Nellie. "They said the Master was going to have story time afterward. I wonder who he will bring this time. I so enjoyed the story about Daniel and the lion at the large event area when we had the stew cook-off. I love the deep timbre of Amra's voice as he talked about being in the presence of God while in the den. It was also fun seeing all of our large animal friends. I love how the Master ties the stories with new recipes showing how everything can work together as planned...like it was supposed to."

"It shows all of us, man and beast, what his divine purpose was, so that we can now learn what needs to be done so that when the time comes, everything will be as it should be," reminded Ruth as she stood and stretched. "Guess it's time to head on back. Wonder if the guys made it back yet and how muddy they are."

"I am sure they will make it back in time for food." Sam chuckled as she also stood to head back to the house. "They are having roasted potatoes and string beans with grilled cheese toast. Hope they have tomatoes as well. Grilled cheese always needs tomatoes."

"You are all about tomatoes, aren't you, Sam?" teased Munchkin.

"Especially if grilled," she added.

Coming back through the arbor, they saw no sign of the guys, so they headed back inside the house. As they entered their main room, the cook poked her head into the room to remind Ruth of the meeting that evening for the upcoming feast and gathering. All heads of the houses met to make sure plans were carried out methodically so that no one was left out that wanted to participate.

A good-hearted ruckus from the front of the house let everyone know the guys were back from their adventure in the creek.

"Hello there," greeted Ruth as they entered the room. "No one looks muddy. Did you actually stay dry?"

OUR HOME OF LOVE

"Jake was there, and we actually just sat on the bank and talked," said Zero. "James was not available, but Jake said he would make sure he told James of your request."

"And I learned something new," remarked Dittims, "how the street and house numbers work."

"Yes," said Ruth. "We would have eventually gotten there, but our initial goal is to get you comfortable with us and for you to hear some of our stories with Christy, and of course, we want to hear yours. There is much to learn for you as well as us."

"I am kind of in learning overload right now." Dittims sighed as he fell onto one of the large cushions. "The fish were really nice, though, and the stream"—he paused in question—"that's also part of the same water source?"

"It is," said Gypsy as she settled on a cushion as well.

"We have a little time before food is ready. Shall we start a story?" said Ruth.

"I believe you are next in line, Ruth," said Gypsy.

Chapter 21

> Nothing makes me smile more than looking into the face of a dog that loves me.

"Well, Dittims," she started, "you and I were there together for a time, so I will lean my stories toward my younger years. There were later times when you, Azer, Gracie, Munchkin, and I were all together. And while those were some great stories, they can be shared at different times or as stories remind us of similar situations anyone can chime in."

Ruth leaned back on her cushion quiet for a moment in memory before she started.

"Let's start at my beginning on the scene. My mother's caretaker understood caring for animals, so when we were still quite young, she was part of an adoption drive at the local dog shelter. The people in the community came out to support the local shelter and to see all the dogs and puppies that needed homes.

"I remember being so frightened of all those people coming by our small fenced-off area that I stayed as far to the back as possible. My three brothers and one sister were all jumping up on the fence, wanting to be picked up and loved on, but I just wanted to run and hide. Then Christy walked by. I remember her reaching down and petting everyone on the fence, but she was watching me. There was such gentleness about her that I was not scared of her as I watched her walked around the fence to see me better. When she picked me up, I just moaned. I was so scared of heights. But she cuddled me close, and all fear went away. Next thing I knew, she was talking to the adoption ladies, and I was adopted."

"For Dittims's sake, Ruth," said Sam, "why don't you go over the time line and a brief history of where Christy was at this point?"

"That's a good idea as it may make my stories a little more understandable about the whys. When I first arrived on the scene, Christy had all three children and was raising them on her own. She and John no longer saw eye to eye on things, so they split their partnership. Christy had not had a longtime pet since living with her parents and being with Sam. She had Dagu in college, and she had Samson for a few months when all the kids were small. But she was not willing to bring a pet into a possible volatile situation."

"Was he a mean person?" asked Dittims.

"No, he just was very frustrated. He had lost his first love."

"First love? I don't understand," asked Dittims.

"The Master," Ruth explained, "should always be our first love, man and beast alike. That's how it was originally created. And sometimes people forget that."

"As I am beginning to understand," said Dittims.

"Now," reminded Ruth, "you see why we start all newcomers out so slow. Let them get their feet wet before we push them fully in the pool."

Soft chuckles and knowing nods went around the room.

"Are you beginning to see why we feel Ruth is so special not only to us but to Christy as well?" explained Munchkin. "She has a stronger insight into the Master's way than some of us do."

"Well," continued Ruth, "two weeks after my adoption, friends at Christy's church who knew she had been looking for a pet and without asking her first brought her another puppy. But Christy would not say no, so there were two of us. Her name was Butterfinger, and about six months later, the youth pastor's dog at the church had puppies, and Christy's youngest fell in love with them, so now there were three. His name was Oreo, a black-and-white cocker mix. The kids had the food group going in pet names."

Dittims looked around the room before asking, "Are they not members of this Love Team?"

"No, they are not. Oreo and Butterfinger decided to make babies together, and they were cuties. A neighborhood lady complained about Christy's ability to properly take care of them all. And one day, while Christy was at work, Oreo, Butterfinger, and all the puppies were stolen from the back porch."

"No way," exclaimed Dittims.

"Yep. About a year later, Christy and her daughter were on a walk in the neighborhood and saw Butterfinger in a fenced-in yard at the back of the same subdivision where they lived."

"Did she go get her?"

"No, Christy is big on 'picking your battles,' and this was one she was not willing to fight at that time. So we are not sure where they are. I am sure we will run into them one day."

"Interesting," thought Dittims.

"But let's back up again to my beginning. Christy had just bought her first house, and the kids had wanted a puppy. The house was located at the bottom end of cul-de-sac, so no fast traffic would zip by the house. The neighborhood was an older quieter area of town with mixed ages of people from small young families to retired couples. It had two main streets coming in and out, so not much through traffic either. It was a wonderful place to walk, and there were lots of nice evening walks. I remember even Tigger, the cat, going with us as we walked, and he was close to twelve years old when I came along. Oh, and for confusion's sake, this is not the same Tigger as the one we spoke of earlier when Christy and John were first married.

"The house had several large oak trees that kept the house shaded during those hot summer days. And in the fall, there were huge piles of leaves that would get raked up and burned weather permitting. I remember Munchkin and I pulling the occasional pecan from a neighbor's tree out of the fire and eating it once it cooled. They were quite tasty. At that time, Christy was driving all the way

OUR HOME OF LOVE

across Atlanta to work, almost an hour one way, which meant she would leave really early before the kids left for school. Christy would rely on her daughter to get herself and the youngest son off to school. The oldest son, Ken, was off at boarding school and doing very well."

"Why was he not living with the rest of the family?" asked Dittims.

"That is a long story for another time," explained Munchkin. "But I will tell you this, when he graduated, he was valedictorian and went from there to college to study airplane mechanics. I lived with him for a while."

"All of Christy's kids are smart," said Ruth, "and they all love dogs. I remember the tenderness I felt with all of those kids. Shortly after they first got me and took me home, the youngest, Rick, would lie on the floor, and I would crawl all over him, and it would make him laugh. I remember how difficult that house was for me to navigate when I was young. The living room and kitchen were on the main level, but the den was downstairs along with the laundry room. All of the bedrooms were upstairs. I remember one afternoon when Christy lost her footing from the upstairs section and sliding down the stair to the main level on her knees. Nothing was broken, but she had some significant bruises. I think part of the issues she now has with her knees was from that fall."

"Well, the ski accident didn't help that any either," commented Sam, "or the antics she did when horseback riding."

"All of us, man and beast alike, suffered with our joints as we grew older a lot of time because of our younger antics."

Knowing nods went around the room.

"What's one of the earliest stories you can remember?" asked Dittims.

"Probably the second porch fire incident from the youngest child. Both boys had a thing for fire."

"I don't remember you speaking about a fire before," commented Sam. "And what do you mean about second fire?"

"Well, everyone knows that boys and sticks or boys and rocks, and sometimes, fire just go together. Boys are just curious creatures. It was late fall, with dry leaves everywhere, and Rick was bored. He had seen his older brother flick matches along the edge of the box which would light them, sending them into the yard. He was standing on the back deck flicking matches to the ground. That section of the yard had very little grass because of the large trees, so he thought nothing about the dangers of a lit match hitting the ground which was normally always dirt. The kids always got home about thirty to forty-five minutes before Christy, and a lot of mischief can happen in a short amount of time. Rick heard Christy drive up, so he quickly put up the matches away thinking she would not know what he had been doing. Unbeknownst to him, the last match did not clear the porch but landed in the leaves on the edge of the porch. Fortunately, the deck is off the kitchen with sliding glass doors, and Christy saw the smoke before any damage was done. Rick got a stern talking to."

"Okay, again," inquired Sam, "what did you mean by second time?"

"Evidently, when Rick was young, he did something similar, but that one involved bringing out the fire department. Even Ken had an issue with fires in the garage that could have been a disaster."

"Boys," said Munchkin, shaking her head.

"But Rick is doing wonderful now. Still playing with fire"—Ruth chuckled—"it's just located on a stove top. He is evidently a fine chef."

"And her daughter Mary is in the restaurant business as well, management, I think," said Munchkin.

"She was," continued Ruth, "but now is in administration for a company who sells computer systems for restaurants."

Ruth thought for a moment.

"I will always have a special place for her in my heart as she watched over me as I gave birth to my only littler of pups. Christy had been very concerned for me thinking I may have cancer because I never showed the classic signs of pregnancy like being fat, but my nipples had gotten hard and swollen. Now understand, I was not a young dog when this happened, so Christy was fearful it was something bad."

"How many babies did you have?" asked Dittims.

"Only three, and Christy was going to keep one because they were from me, but it just did not happen. Too many people wanted one."

"You went everywhere with Christy. So tell about some of your rides," prodded Munchkin, "and the drive-through stories."

Ruth chuckled as she continued. "Anytime Christy was going on a short errand, I always got to go, like to the bank, the burger joint, or ice cream parlor. And I always got a treat. The ice cream parlor was my favorite. I got my own cup that fit right in the vans cup holder. But even the bank had biscuits in a jar for people who had their dogs with them."

"Oh, I remember bank trips too." Dittims spoke up. "Christy had a pickup with an extended cab. That is where I rode, and I would stick my head out her window. People would be shocked about a dog of my size in the backseat. I took up the entire back. Christy would also open the small back window, and I would stick my head out there when riding down the highway. You didn't get the heavy wind factor like with a side window. People would just laugh and smile."

"People love to see dogs in cars," said Sam. "I remember even in my day, people got a real kick out of it."

"So did you go with her all the time?" asked Dittims.

"Once I got older, and the kids were gone, but there is a lot to talk about before we got to that point."

After a brief pause, Ruth remembered back and continued.

"Let's start back at the beginning again. We really jump around sometimes and get ahead of the time line. You see, Dittims, some of us have heard the stories we tell with each new member, and we all have developed favorites. Even when there is no one new, we get together with friends of other houses and share each other's stories. It's a way that we stay connected, not only with Christy and her memory but with each other.

"Let's talk about the hurricane story. As Nellie told you, sometimes when there is a big hurricane that comes through the gulf, it can stay as a tropical storm, as it moves through the upper states. This particular storm caused damage again at the Florida house, and as it curved through Georgia, it was still a strong storm with high winds and torrential rain. There was a large pine tree right outside of Mary's bedroom that split in half and fell catching the window as it slide down the side of the house. Fortunately, only the screen was damaged, but we did lose power for several days due to downed power lines. The storm moved from our area on over to the East Coast and then traveled up the coast, causing much damage to roads all the way up through Virginia. There were even some coastal roads that were completely destroyed."

"Since you had no power, did you stay at the house?" asked Dittims.

"It was a late storm that occurred in early fall, so the temperatures were not that hot. It forced people in the neighborhoods to be outside more, though. Taking walks since you could not watch TV and cooking meals on grills. And it was on a weekend, so Christy didn't have to go to work."

"Weather can be a fearful thing in more than one form. Remember the tornado scares we had when we were in Alabama?" reminded Dittims.

"Yes, and Christy is in the Midwest now, where they are even more frequent."

"I thought it odd at first that she moved a thousand miles away from family when she moved to the Midwest," commented Gypsy, "but she really seems to like it. She is getting back into some fun stuff like clowning and face painting."

"If I remember correctly," chimed in Nellie, "all of those activities started at the Georgia house just as the kids were finishing high school and heading off to college."

"Oh, it looks like food is ready," said Ruth. "This is a good stopping spot, and I think Dittims needs an overload break as well. We can pick back up tomorrow."

Chapter 22

> Heaven is where all the dogs you've ever
> loved come to greet you upon arrival.

For the first time since his arrival, Dittims was the last one to wake up. The room was empty, but he heard gentle voices outside, and after stretching, he headed to join them.

"Oh, look," teased Munchkin, "he lives."

"Sorry I slept so long. Guess it finally caught up with me."

"You have had a lot of info thrown at you the last couple of days. You survived the initial onslaught, and now things will start to fall into rhythm where you can process at your own rate. The first week is the hardest, but you did great."

"Well, breakfast will be ready soon, and we can decide if we are ready for more stories after that," said Ruth.

"I have a better idea," sounded a voice from around the corner of the house.

"Skeebo," hailed Zero as Skeebo joined the group.

"I just left Spot and Rusty at the community center where they are gathering friends for a Pack Day."

"We have not had a Pack Day in a good while. That is a good idea," chimed in Munchkin.

"Spot thought it would be a good thing for Dittims so he could meet more of us."

"What is Pack Day?" asked Dittims.

"It's the day we get to size you up for games," said Zero.

"Oh, so this is game day?"

"Sort of," explained Ruth. "Game day is a lot bigger with lots of people and pets of all kinds, but Pack Day is just for dogs with a few people that want to participate. It will be a good diversion for you."

"Okay," said Dittims, "I am in, but why is it called Pack Day?"

"Sorry, Dittims," teased Munchkin, "but, *duh*, a group of dogs is a pack."

"Ah." Dittims nodded as everyone was chuckling at his expense.

"Not everything," continued Skeebo, "has a deep meaning. Sometimes, it's just basic stuff."

"Well then, Pack Day it is," affirmed Ruth. "Skeebo, have you had breakfast?"

"Not really. I grabbed a fig as I left Spot's."

"Then stay for breakfast, and we can all go together."

"Sounds like a good plan."

After eating, the nine Love Team members headed together toward the community center in wonder of who all would be there. Sometimes, these smaller events are more comfortable for the newcomers or friends who just did not like large crowds. As the group left their street and got on the main road for the area, they could see numerous friends also heading to the community center.

"Hey, Rusty, Samwise, wait up," called Zero as he ran ahead to walk with them.

"Gosh," said Dittims more to himself than really talking to anyone, "they look like twins except for the size difference."

"Yes," affirmed Ruth. "Rusty is a full-sized collie, and Samwise is a sheltie. Samwise is great for games as he is fast. If Charlie shows up, they will make a formidable team. Charlie is a shepherd mix and also very fast as well."

"I am hoping someone brings bubbles. I love the bubble bust game," said Sandra as she jumped in the air, pretending to pop bubbles.

OUR HOME OF LOVE

"While I do enjoy the games," said Gracie, "I prefer to be on the sideline and watch."

"I enjoy the visiting. Dittims, this will be a good chance to get to know some friends better, dog and people," reminded Ruth.

As they entered the main commons area, some games were already in play. On the far side, they had Frisbee setup with some foam balls getting set up near the pool of the creek. At quick glance, there were close to thirty already present with more coming in.

"I see Muffin over there with another basset, and I think that is Matilda," said Sam. "I have not seen her in quite a while. I am going to go say hi."

"Come on, Dittims," said Azer as he nudged his brother. "I see Jake over there near the Frisbee toss. I really think you could do well over there. Let's go see."

"Well, Gracie, I think you had a great idea," said Ruth. "Let's go park ourselves over there on the knoll. We should be able to see most of the playing field from up there."

As they found a suitable spot on the knoll, the grounds were teaming with fun and energy as numerous game and agility courses got set up across the wide center grounds. Two separate games of Frisbee were in the center with various ball-chasing games along the sides. Sandra was in her on world with the bubble pop set up near the tables where someone brought in a large cushion so that they could bound off the table into the air to land on a soft place.

"Hello, may I join you?" asked Tip as she climbed the knoll.

"Only if you plan on laughing with us as we watch the antics going on down there." Ruth chuckled as she welcomed her friend.

"That can easily be arranged. What all do we have going on this time?"

"Have you met my brother Dittims? He is trying to learn about Frisbee. He is in the far group."

"Yes, I did. That could be real interesting. He is bigger than you."

"I am curious to know what they are doing by the creek," wondered Ruth. "You have Dagu, Sampson, Zero, Trouble, and Blacky. Those guys are all ball chasers. Not sure why Blacky is with them."

"I heard them talking when I walked by there, and she is just a referee. They have a short net set up in the shallows of the creek, and two teams are playing with the foam balls. I think they are waiting on more players."

"Okay, that makes more sense," said Ruth.

"Oh, look, there is Brownie and Whoopsy going against Trip and Nellie on one of the ball strategy courses," said Tip.

"Where did Sam get to?" said Gracie. "Oh, I see them over at the ring drop."

"That's funny." Ruth laughed. "You have the lazy bassets dropping the rings down the slide to the herders and sprinters who are racing them back to the top to be dropped again."

"The bassets I think I know. That's Sam, Muffin, and Matilda, right? But I don't know the guys at the bottom," said Tip.

"The husky is Skeebo. He is part of our Love Team, and the two Australian shepherds are brother and sister, Val and Gracie."

"I see James and his crew are here as usual, making sure everything is set up correctly, but I don't recognize the guy by the gate or his dog," said Gracie.

"Oh my, I think that may be Oreo," said Ruth, and she got up. "Be right back."

"Someone she knows?" asked Tip.

"I think it may be an old lost member to the team, not sure."

Tip and Gracie watched as Ruth met the newcomer with obvious recognition; then their attention was drawn to the commotion in the center as several groups were cheering on the last leg of the ball switch concourse with team Buddy and Brownie being neck and neck with team Whoopsy and Bugsy. James declared both teams in a tie as they all broke through the ribbon at the same time.

"Great race, you guys," said James. "It's been a fun afternoon for all. My crew is laying out watermelon for everyone, and there is plenty of freshwater scattered about the grounds. Relax and enjoy each other's company, and meet friends you have not met yet."

The guys who had been playing foam ball in the creek were lying in the center area, getting dry. The bassets were heading toward melon tables, and the high-energy friends were still playing Frisbee.

OUR HOME OF LOVE

Ruth was taking her old friend around to introduce him to the Love Team. It was great finding an old acquaintance and renewing the friendship.

"Hey, Dittims," said Azer, "you did pretty good today. Your jump is high, but you need to perfect your timing. You will get there."

"Thanks. Let's go get some water. I am parched."

"Hey, Dittims and Azer," called Ruth from across the way, "I have someone you need to meet."

As they met near one of the watering pools, Ruth introduced her friend.

"Remember on the first or second day, we were talking about Christy's dogs and puppies getting stolen from her porch. This is Oreo. Oreo, these are some of the Love Team members. Dittims is our newest member."

"It's great to meet you," said Dittims. "Do you still go by Oreo?"

"Actually, I do. I know that is usually not the case, but it was for me."

"You will have to come share your stories sometime."

"I will. But for right now, I think we are leaving. We have a meeting set up in a different sector. I will try to get by soon."

"How neat was that? We were just talking about him. Does he know where any of the others were taken?"

"I did not ask. He said he was living over in District 62," said Ruth. "That will be a fun story time."

When the games finally stopped, everyone circled up and visited for a while before heading home.

"Well, Dittims," asked Ruth, "how are you feeling after your first game experience? You seemed to be able to handle the Frisbee pretty easily."

"Well, I don't know how easy it was, but it was definitely fun. And I met another newcomer, not as new as me but more recent than anyone else that I had talked to. His name was Trouble, black-and-white shepherd mix I think."

"Yes, Trouble is fairly new. He was playing with us in in the creek. He is very good with the ball," said Zero.

"I may need a nap when we get home," said Dittims. "While that was fun, it can be tiring."

"Sounds like a great idea to me," said Sam as they turned down Fifty-First Street.

"Napping is your specialty," teased Munchkin.

And the group settled in peaceful companionship as they headed to the house.

Chapter 23

*Regardless of how bad your day was, there is
a wagging tail waiting for you to get home.*

After a short nap, Dittims was fully refreshed and ready for whatever came his way. Sam and Nellie were still resting, so Dittims headed out back. No one seemed to be in the back, so he turned to head toward the front. As he rounded the perennial corner of the house, he saw Ruth, Jake, and Gypsy with James standing by the raised bed they had talked about for possible upgrades.

"Afternoon, everyone."

"Hey, Dittims," said James, "how did you enjoy your first game party? You seem to do pretty well with the Frisbee."

"I am working on it. It was lots of fun, and I met lots of new friends. We even ran across an old team member."

"Really!"

"Yes," explained Ruth. "The tall gentleman that came toward the end of the games with the black-and-white cocker mix, that was Oreo, originally on our team."

"Oh yea. That was David. He is the head garden keeper like me over in District 62, where they are having that massive renovation. He came by to see our Pack Day. They are thinking of putting in a section for a permanent obstacle courses. Since they don't have a stream running through their community center, they have more land area."

"Did y'all decide on what to do here?" asked Dittims.

"Yes," confirmed Ruth, "we have a beginning idea that may be tweaked as it goes."

"Okay," said James, "I will get it scheduled and let you know approximate timing."

"Thank you, James," said Ruth as he turned to leave.

"Sure thing, I will be in touch."

"So," Ruth asked, looking at Dittims, "how are we feeling? Ready for more stories?"

"Sure."

"Let's head down to the pond," suggested Gypsy. "They finished that work, and I have not had a chance to enjoy it yet. Some of the angel trumpets are already opening up."

"Zero, Skeebo, and Azer are helping Bill Jones with the final stages of a short project. They will be along shortly," commented Ruth as they headed down the slight slope to the pond.

As they were getting settled on the benches, they saw Sam and Nellie heading their way.

"Y'all look like you were having fun earlier," said Ruth. "Nellie, I saw you and Trip do real well. Y'all are well matched in speed."

"I am partial to the ring slide game. All I have to do is sit." Sam chuckled. "Dittims, you seemed to have fun with the Frisbee. You had some pretty high jumps."

"Need to learn a little more finesse, but I am getting there."

"Shall we begin another set of stories?" asked Ruth.

"I kind of forgot where we were," commented Nellie.

"Well, we have talked about my first home and me having babies, but I think it's time to move to on to the Virginia house. Christy's job had been located near the Atlanta airport, but the owner was from Virginia, and he wanted to move the company there. Some of the employees were offered to move there as well, and Christy was ready for a change. The older kids were in college, but Rick was in a boarding school in Virginia, so she took this opportunity to be a little closer to him. She found a cute little house with a great view of the mountains, and it was surrounded by pasture land. I loved it, great place for me to run and play. And it was so beautiful when it snowed except the driveway was too steep for snow travel. There was a garage down at the bottom of the hill for parking when the snows came."

Ruth leaned back, remembering some of her experiences in the snow.

"While there were quite a few snow stories, I have to first tell you about an event that happened shortly after she moved in. The layout of the house was rectangular with entry on one side and bedrooms on the opposite end. The living was long and almost covered the full length of the house with two bedrooms closing off the end and separated by the bathroom. The dining room was where the view was. Both outside walls were banked with tall windows for viewing the mountains. Christy loved to sit there and enjoy the view as she ate. She got up early one morning just before sunrise and was setting her plate down on the table when she noticed the trees on the far mountain looked to be on fire, and as she watched, she saw the fire was growing. She was in a state not knowing what to do if anything. She didn't know who to call or how to describe where this fire was located, so she just stood rooted watching it increase and talked to me like I could do anything about it. Its size and brightness increased until the truth hit her full in the face, literally. It was not a fire but was the sun cresting the mountain as it rose. With the trees being empty of leaves as it was late fall, the light seeped through them and indeed looked like a fire. This became a favorite morning enjoyment as she studied her Bible verses and ate her breakfast."

"Wow." Dittims chuckled. "But can you imagine if it really was a fire. Fires in mountains can be hard to fight."

"Hey, Ruth," teased Gypsy, "this is the house where you did your leap of death, isn't it?"

Ruth moaned to herself and softly chuckled knowing each one of them had "that story" that made everyone laugh.

"Yes, it is, but it needs a little background information for Dittims. The house in Georgia had woods and a swampy-type area behind it, so all kinds of local wildlife would walk through the back of the yard, including the unmentionables. That area of Georgia had lots of opossums, so if one of those lovely creatures would enter the yard, I would give chase. They are fairly slow and easy to catch, and I would grab them by the neck and shake them until they were dead or at least played dead, which they are known for. Then I could walk off as the hero. I save the family from creature of the lagoon," mocked Ruth in a deep rough voice.

"Ah, the hero story," teased Zero as he, Azer, and Skeebo returned from helping at the farm.

"Yes," confirmed Ruth, "we all have our moments."

Loving laughter echoed from the pond as good friends enjoyed each other's company.

"Okay, so how does this fit in with the Virginia house?" asked Dittims.

"The most used entry to this house was off the side by the driveway with a raised porch, and you entered into a small entryway off the living room. That porch was about three feet off the ground on the front side of the house. One warm sunny day, as we were going outside, I caught a whiff of something from the front yard. There was a three-foot-high wall around the porch to assure no one would fall off the porch. I placed my paws on the front edge of that wall, and the scent was so strong I did not think, and before I knew it, I cleared that wall to the ground and dove into the shrubs going for a critter."

"Did you get hurt?" asked Dittims. "What did Christy do?"

"She was scared for me knowing how far I had jumped and that I was not a young dog anymore. But since it did not seem to bother me and that I was still in pursuit, she knew it was something real that I was after. Skunks were prevalent in the area as I found out the hard way, and she thought I had another skunk. Oh, FYI—tomato juice does help some, and we kept it on hand. Anyway, Christy came around to see what I was after, and whatever it was, it had gotten trapped in the plastic tubing that came off the downspout for the front corner of the house. Christy was trying to keep me at bay as she pulled the tubing off the downspout, but in the process, out rolled a baby opossum from the tube. I did my due diligence by shaking to assure it was dead and again saved the world."

OUR HOME OF LOVE

"And how long was it before it got up and walked off?" asked Skeebo as all were laughing as they visualized the scene.

"About forty-five minutes."

"If I remember correctly from all the stories that we have told," said Gypsy, "none of us have critter stories other than the unmentionables that we are not going to mention."

"I think you are right. Shows how special I am"—chucked Ruth—"except for Dittims, whom we have not heard yet, and Mimi has a funny story that the Master was telling me about involving a raccoon on the roof."

"What other stories in Virginia do you have?" asked Dittims.

"I have an activity we loved, not really a story. The garage at the bottom of the hill was nestled at the back into the side of the hill, making the roof an easy access for climbing onto. You just stepped onto it from the hill. We loved to go there and sit on the roof together and watch the sunset."

"Oh, that is neat," said Dittims. "Did you have other activities you liked doing there?"

"Not really. Christy mostly worked all the time and was a homebody when she did come home, but something happened at work that bothered her. Nor sure what it was, but she felt like it was time to go back to Georgia. By this time, she had gotten you Skeebo from a litter of her daughter's dog, so I will leave further mountain stories for you. Georgia would always be her home state I think regardless of where she went. Her oldest kids were now finished with school, and the youngest was in college in North Carolina, so she decided to move back to Georgia. She got a new job not far from where she spent most of her early adult life, just outside of Atlanta. While that job did not last long due to the economy, it did afford her the job opportunity for Alabama where she was for about nine years. It got her back close to home near her brother and sisters since her mom were not in the best of health."

"I remember you talking about that move from Virginia. Christy did all the packing by herself, and a couple of friends from work came to help her load the heavy stuff on the rental truck," said Gypsy.

"Yes, that was a move to remember," said Ruth softly. "You had a single woman in her midforties driving the largest rental truck available while pulling her car behind her for a twelve-hour drive. Skeebo and I were in the front seat, and Kitty was in a cat carrier behind the seat."

"Did the trip go okay?" asked Dittims.

"Only had one mishap of getting stuck at a gas station, but wonderful people helped her get straight, and we were on our way again. We went to Val and Gracie family's house. And those friends help Christy get settled."

"And you said you were not there long?" asked Dittims.

"Comparatively no, but a lot happened as she bought her dream home. Christy had hoped to grow old in this last house and share great times with her friends, but God had other plans. Christy was there for only about a year and a half, but so much happened there. She and her friends got in the clowning business together. Then all three kids came home to regroup as their lives momentarily went belly up, and they brought all of their dogs with them."

"How big was this house?" asked Dittims, thinking of all the people and animals in one house.

"Pretty big. It had three bedrooms one end with a separate dining room and living room, plus a huge country kitchen. Then there was an addition of a suite with a bedroom, kitchen, living room, and a huge game room downstairs."

"Nice."

"Well, as with any older home, there were always issues. And then Christy got laid off, and she could not find work locally, so she had to shop out of state and found work in Alabama."

"What about all the people in the house and their dogs?" asked Dittims.

"Well, let's back up a bit and go into detail of that time line. When they first arrived, Christy was in a tiny rental house, but she and the leasing person knew this was short time while she looked for a house to purchase. The only story worth talking about belongs to Skeebo, and while it is gross, I will let him tell you about it."

OUR HOME OF LOVE

"I didn't think it was gross," defended Skeebo. "It's just who I was."

"Well, your teammates can be the judge of that, I just remember us ladies not really approving."

"Now my curiosity is up," said Dittims.

"In due time," continued Ruth. "It was not long before Christy found this large house hoping to be a base for her, her friends, and the clowning business. About four months after buying the house, Mary moved home to rethink her relationship with her boyfriend. And she brought Lakota, Skeebo's mom, along with Lucy, an American bulldog, and two cats."

"Good grief," exclaimed Dittims. "That's a lot of animals for one person."

"Oh, it gets better. A month later, both boys moved home, and each brought a dog, one of which was Munchkin. And remember the suite where her friends were living? They had Val and Gracie."

"It was rather chaotic if I remember," said Munchkin as she and Sandra joined the group. "Ken was dog sitting for a friend in the military while he was overseas, so Butch was not with us long but still it was another dog."

"Hey, how was your visit with Daphne? Is she doing any better?" asked Ruth.

"Yea, I was surprised to see her go to Pack Day. She said she needed a diversion. That's why Sandra and I stayed a while with her."

"For those of you who don't know Daphne, she is new, and, Dittims, while it is wonderful here, we still care and pray for those we left."

"Back to story time," said Munchkin, "it sounds like you are talking about one of my favorite houses, with the apple trees?"

Ruth nodded in amusement. "Yes, your trees as we called them. I was just explaining about the dynamics of the house. The kids did not stay too long either. Rick was only there for about three months. Then he went to culinary school in Atlanta and found a place of his own. And Mary made up with her boyfriend about six months later, and he moved all of them back to Virginia, so it was just Christy and Ken and the black dogs. Rick had left Munchkin with Ken as he was not able to have him in his new living situation. It was not too long after that when Christy lost her job. So now she had a new house with payments she could not afford without a job, so she had to find work. It took another four months and an out-of-state search, but she final found a job in Alabama. She tried to commute for a couple of weeks, but it just was too much, so she found a rental house. As much as she didn't want to sell the house, she had no choice. She could not afford rent and mortgage, and then the market crashed, and she was not able to sell it. Her friends had told her to just let it go, but her father had trained her that you don't run from your responsibilities. But then the accident happened, and she had no choice but to let it go. Her friends had already moved out, so the house was sitting empty."

"The accident was during my time frame," said Dittims softly in remembrance. "It was a scary time as I didn't have a clue what was happening."

"I think now might be a good time for a break as my stories are about done because we are overlapping each other. I will go check on food, and then afterward, we can resume. And as I have said before, lots of stories will come to mind as we spend our time here, and we can share them then. The famous story of Munchkin and I and the snake came while we were living in this house, and we have already talked about it. And we have touched on Munchkin and her love of apples from this house. Skeebo, we have not talked about you at all, and you started with me in Virginia, so maybe it is your turn to do a bit of back tracking for you to bring us up to date for this house before we start the Alabama stories."

"That sounds like the logical plan, but I don't have a lot of stories since my accident happened at the Georgia house that brought me here."

"That's true," said Ruth. "We are actually getting close to you, Dittims, and I am really looking forward to that."

Chapter 24

*Sometimes, the best medicine is a dog
who thinks his love can cure you.*

After eating, the Love members settled on their cushions in the main room for a continuation of where they had left off earlier. Skeebo was setting his cushion more centered for all to hear him well as Spot entered the room.

"I was hoping to catch Dittims as he started. I am interested in his new stories."

"Almost," said Ruth. "We are actually with Skeebo and doing a little back tracing since there was overlapping times between me and the rest of the team including Dittims."

"I forgot about that," remembered Spot. "The overlap started in Virginia and lasted through Alabama, didn't it?"

"Yes, it did," affirmed Skeebo. "I started it when Christy got me from Mary. Lakota is my mom as y'all know, and I got to be with mom some in Georgia when Mary came down to live with her mom and the rest of the crew that came back home for a spell."

"Yes," agreed Ruth, "lots of fur in one house."

Nods and snickers floated through the room.

"Okay, let me help Dittims understand about me and my breed. Huskies are the closest dog to the original wolf, where all of us originate from, and some of us, as in me, have traits that are closer to the wolf that an average domesticated dog. This is a draw for some people that love the husky breed but a detriment for people like Christy, who like for us to be able to run free. Our ancestral instincts are too strong to allow that, and that is what got me in trouble. But let's start at the beginning. When Christy first got me, she put me in a cage to take me home as she lived on the opposite side of the state from Mary. She had the seats in her van down, and the cage was where she could reach over and console me, but I was not going to be consoled. I sat in the middle of that cage and howled for my mom the entire way home. Other drivers on the highway would see me, and I would look at them and howl even more. They just laughed at me. At that time, I didn't understand what was so funny. Now I kinda do. But when we got to the house, it was better because I had Ruth there to comfort me. She had been in the front seat the entire time, but I was too scared to notice she was even there. The first couple of months were great as we would go outside, and I could run free as I wanted. Then one afternoon, I went too far and ended up down the road at a neighbor's house. That is where I met King, and that is when everything for me changed, and Christy could no longer control me if I got loose. King was a true wolf that had been injured, and these people took care of injured wildlife and reintroduced them back into the wild. But King was too injured to ever return, so he stayed with them. He didn't have but three legs, and his lungs were too damaged to release him. Whenever I got loose, that is where I would go. The stories he would tell would just ignite my wild side, and mine was stronger than my siblings'. When we moved to Georgia, Christy had a section of the yard fenced in so that I could still be turned loose but be safe. But the fence was no match for me. Christy realized it when I climbed over the fence and was gone for two days. She thought I was gone for good, but I brought her a present, half a deer carcass."

"That is so gross," said Nellie. "You got hooked up with coyotes for those two days if I remember correctly."

"I don't understand why you would do that," said Dittims.

"It's what my wild instincts pulled me toward combined with the stories I had heard from King, and now I had real wild friends."

OUR HOME OF LOVE

"What did Christy do?" asked Dittims.

"She knew now that I had tasted wild game, there was no stopping me if I got loose, so she added a chain inside the fence to keep me from climbing out. And that worked fine until one day I got loose again and did not see the car as I zoomed across the road to freedom. I just didn't not know what real freedom was until I got here. It took several sessions with the Master to make me understand the truth and what his plans for me were. And Dittims, the love of this team and this place really make you understand just how lucky all of us are."

"Were you the only one who came here in that fashion, I mean those who I have talked to talked about getting sick before coming here?"

"Sort of. I was the only one who came here through my own selfish recklessness. But it gives me a different perspective and truth. God really does use all instances for good. You may not see it at first, but if you look back, he uses each one of us differently accordingly to our experiences. I have been able to work with people who have gotten here through tragic instances and help them to adjust. Everything is used according to God's plan. The plan may change at any given moment, but it always comes to good."

Dittims looked around the room in wonder and awe as Skeebo's story sunk in.

"It makes me wonder about me. I did nothing special. I had vision and hearing issues."

"That's because you don't see what we see," said Ruth, "and I think what the Master sees. Give it some time, Dittims. You have only been here a couple of weeks."

"Okay."

"Well, Munchkin. I do believe we are down to you, and after you, it's the big guys." Spot chuckled.

"I guess my story started with Christy as she purchased me as a gift for her youngest child, Rick. While I look like a black lab, my dad was actually a chocolate lab, which can explain my fun personality."

Everyone laugh knowing she could be real ditzy at times.

"I am not sure your breeding explains your happy-go-lucky personality," teased Sandra.

"Probably not, but it sounds good. Anyway, I was not with Christy at first but did spend the last five years with her until I met with a similar careless decision like Skeebo's bringing me here before any natural health issues. The house in Georgia was on a larger piece of land with many woods to explore, and those were the most fun. Christy would take us on long walks exploring the property and letting us run free. Skeebo, you and I had some great adventures in those woods."

"Yea, remember that tree that had fallen and hung out over hill? It was great fun to walk down and jump off of."

"You were more of a daredevil on stuff like that than I was. I remember some long walks going all the way down to the creek with Rick as well. We have already talked about the fun adventure in the state part with Rick, Christy, and the unmentionable. That was about the only story I had for Georgia other than the apple trees we have also already discussed. When Rick decided to go back to school, I was not allowed to go with him. So I stayed with Christy, Ken, and Mary. Mary moved next as she went back to Virginia. When Christy moved to Alabama, Ken and I stayed at the Georgia house for a while, but the drive for his work got to be too expensive as gas prices were crazy, so he moved closer to work. That is when I went to stay with Christy and Ruth in Alabama. At first, we were in a little rental house until she found the place near her work to purchase. It was a neat place. It made you feel like you were way out in the country but really only twenty minutes from town. It was not as big as the place in Georgia but still had lots of room to run free. Plus there was a small pond on the property."

"Oh, I loved that pond," said Dittims. It had a path all the way around it that you could walk around."

"Which you never seemed to use," teased Ruth. "Since it was shallow during the dry season, you would run across it getting nasty muddy."

"Like I said, I loved that pond," said Dittims as everyone laughed, picturing this large animal running across a shallow pond.

OUR HOME OF LOVE

"Remember the year that it snowed Ruth," continued Munchkin. "While it was not what you normally think of snow, but in Alabama, a good ground covering was a lot. Ruth and I would run chasing the flakes as they fell, and I remember how quiet it was. Normally, the road that ran by the house was very busy, but it was a Saturday, and nobody was going anywhere much."

Munchkin thought a moment before continuing. "The property was divided into three separate areas of exploration. You had the pond which had a path and evergreen trees around. You had the front pasture that was by the road. Then there was the main part where the house and three raised flower beds were. Christy always planted a few vegetables along with the rosemary that was already there."

"Remember the time you got into the pepper plant?" said Ruth.

"Not a fun time. I stayed away from the garden after that. It was during the year that Christy went and brought Mary home from Virginia for good, along with the crew, Lakota, Lucy, and the two cats, Scarlett and Miss Precious."

"That had to have been an interesting trip," said Dittims.

"Yes," continued Munchkin. "Mary's car was packed with animals, so all of her stuff was packed in Christy's pickup, and it was packed like the Beverly Hillbilly's truck heading to California. Sorry, Dittims, I know you do not understand that reference. Just take my word for it. It was overfull."

"Mary, Lakota, and the cats moved with Christy and me when we moved to Iowa," said Dittims. Lucy, Ruth, and you had already come here. But even with this many, I understand being overfull."

Munchkin looked over at Ruth a moment before continuing. "Ruth, I hope you know how much you were missed and loved not only by Christy but the rest of us as well. When you got sick and came here, I lost a best friend, Dittims lost a comforting guide, and Christy, well, she was pretty devastated."

"I know. And I love all of you too. And think how wonderful it is going to be when she gets here," said Ruth almost in tears.

"Ruth, how long were you with Christy?" asked Dittims.

"Almost sixteen years."

The room grew quiet for a moment as each member quickly thought on some special moments they shared with Christy.

"Munchkin, do you have more stories for now?" asked Ruth.

"No not really. We all know my famous story which Ruth was part of."

"Gracie, you usually don't say much. You want to have a go at story time?"

"I was there for such a short time, but I guess you can say I help Dittims survive longer," she said.

"The family who owned the property prior to Christy had raised Dobermans. For some reason, that area was notorious for parvovirus in Dobermans, and parvo can stay alive in the soil for a long time. It never affected you other guys because you were older and your vaccinations had made you strong, but puppies do not have that advantage, and that is what got me. Even though I got sick early, I still felt the love and caring of Christy. She had such a gentle touch. When she lost me, she got with her vet, and he explained to her what she needed to do for her property, and she did that. Then when she found out another set of puppies were coming, she made arrangements with them to keep Dittims and Azer until all vaccinations were completed and tested to make sure they took."

"So you did not get much time for stories, did you?" asked Dittims. "And, Azer, you were sick even before we went to be with Christy."

"That's true, but I did get a little more time with Christy than Gracie did. Do you remember the head butt?"

"Yes, I saw stars."

"Remember how Dittims said he had vision problems?" continued Azer. "He was totally blind on his left side. I was too young to understand that, but, Ruth, you understood that, didn't you?"

"Yes, I did, but you boys were so rambunctious. I tried to make Dittims understand to go slow to accommodate for it, but that never worked."

"We were outside racing each other around the bushes because we do like to run, and I came around from the left as Dittims was turning to the right, and we hit head to head. I yelped in pain, and

OUR HOME OF LOVE

Dittims just sat on his haunches looking dazed. Kind of like how I bet Nellie felt when she hit the laundry room door."

"Not a fun experience," affirmed Nellie.

"I always wondered if that accident is what caused you to get sicker," commented Dittims.

"I don't think that had anything to do with it. You know several of us in our litter had health issues. Your blindness comes from your eye not forming completely. Stacy, our larger sister, had heart issues. My issues were with my guts, and all but one of our littermates plus you got to be full grown dogs. I think it was just too much strain on mom to have a litter so soon after Gracie's litter. So you and Ruth are the only two of us who really got to spend adult time with Christy. Let's finally hear some of your stories."

"Well, we have talked about my favorite game of cup toss and my love to run through the pond. I will start my stories after Ruth and Munchkin had already come here. Let's talk about the only major story for Alabama, Christy's accident, and…the intervention."

"Intervention?" asked Spot.

"That's what Christy called it—her angelic intervention, but let's start at the beginning. Off the back of the house was a nice covered deck, but the steps were not covered. That summer, it had rained a lot. And with no sun hitting those steps to dry them out due to the large oak trees, which make wonderful shade, the steps got slimy. Every day, Christy came home for lunch as she was only ten minutes from work. And she always walked everybody. But Lakota had to be on a leash as Christy had already learned from having Skeebo. As Christy was coming out the door to the deck, her cell phone from work rang, and she pulled it out of her pocket to answer it, and that distracted her for her descent from the deck. She hit the slippery steps and went flying, literally. She landed on her left arm, but the energy of her fall made her slide on the wet leaves, pulling her arm behind her. She had dropped her phone and the leash, but Lakota got tangled in bushes, so she just sat down. Lucy ran off to do her business, and I just watched Christy trying to figure why she was on the ground and not getting up. She sat up and was looking for her phone that she had dropped but didn't see it. She scooted on her bottom to climb back on the porch trying to get in standing position. Once on the bottom step, she saw where her phone had landed, so she retrieved it and called for help. She called her boss first, and since he was coming back from lunch himself, he came straight to her house. He was able to get Lakota and me in the house, but Lucy was on walkabout. He was going to take Christy to the hospital as he also agree her arm was broken, but she told him she had already called 911, and they were on the way. And of course, when they got there, Lucy thought they came to see her, so she was visiting with everybody. They got Lucy in the house as they were putting Christy in the ambulance. Mary had been called at work and was going to meet them at the hospital. They did not get home until dark, so it was a longer than wanted time at the hospital.

"When Christy went back for her checkup a week later, they realized the damage was worse than first realized, so they consulted a specialist for elbows, and surgery had to be done to correct the damage. She was out of work for three months."

"Why did they not realize the severity of the damage?" asked Ruth.

"The X-ray did not show that all of tendons had been ripped loose from the bones. So even though they reset the bones, they would not stay because the tendons were not attached and secure to hold them in place. Plus a piece of bone was shattered off and shifted down in her arm that needed to be removed."

"We had been informed of an accident but did not realize the extent," said Sam. "Where did the angelic intervention come in?" asked Sandra.

"That's what Christy calls it because she said physics could not explain her location after the fall. Now when they told Christy it would be two weeks before they could do the surgery because of a scheduling issue, Christy made a deal with her work to just be present—not to lift anything but to supervise, since indeed that was her job, as quality supervisor, and they agreed. Her hand looked really fat from all the swelling, and her coworkers were surprised that she came to work at all. Mary called it her marshmallow hand as it looked like the Staypuff guy."

OUR HOME OF LOVE

"Oh, I remember the *Ghost Busters* movie with that character," said Munchkin as other joined in with snickers.

"Anyway, when Christy was dressing for work for the first day, she noticed her right hip was very sore, and she got Mary to help her look at it. There was a very large bluish-black deep tissue bruise on her right hip. She wondered what she had hit since she knew she had hit on her left side. So after work, she went back down the steps to see what she hit."

"Not those same slippery steps?" asked Gypsy.

"No, let me tell you about those. When her church found out what had happened, they came and replaced her steps."

"How wonderful! Were those her angels?" Spot asked.

"Not the ones we are talking about, but yes, those members were angels to do that for her. When Christy came down the stairs, she looked all over the area for something that she hit hard enough to make that bruise, and she didn't see anything. Then she started studying the area. She had remembered the mark she left on the step with her shoe was straight, which with normal physics would bring her down on top of the steps, possibly causing further damage. She remembered she was tilting to her left side as she fell, but she landed on the wet leaves of the grass where she slid. She looked again at the area and noticed the grass area where she landed was past the concrete planter that sat on the small brick patio just to the left side of the concrete sidewalk a good four feet from the steps. When Mary got home, they studied the area together, and they came up with the same conclusion. Christy was kicked out of the way of getting further hurt which caused the deep bruise."

"By who?" they said together, knowing there was no one there.

"Her guardian angel," said Dittims quietly.

Deep gasped were heard around the room as everyone was reminded of God's infinite care of his people.

"Ain't God good?" said Spot softly.

"All the time," said Ruth.

"Wow!" said Munchkin softly. "I know you have more stories, but after that, I need a break, maybe some praise and worship time."

"I agree," said Ruth. "We have lots of time for more stories, but maybe now is a good time to reflect on how God is always in control even when you don't see it."

And with that, they quietly left the room going in different directions to find their own quiet place to reflect on the ever-unfolding plan of God. Dittims sat rooted to his cushion as he was thinking on something Ruth had said when he first got there.

Chapter 25

> Don't be sorry. I will wait for you at the
> Rainbow Bridge—Love, your dog

The following morning, Dittims woke early as had become his normal routine. He quietly scooted out the front door to go relax by the pond. As he got to the pond, he saw that Ruth was already there enjoying the pond.

"Good morning."

"Good morning, Dittims. How are you feeling this morning?"

"I am feeling good. I hope my story did not upset anyone. That was not my intention."

"You did not at all. What you did is remind us of a truth that we sometimes forget here. When we are here and sometimes even when working hand in hand with God on a project, we forget this is not how it always was. And your story reminded us that even though people do not see God, and even those that do not believe, he does intervene with us. Sometimes we only can see it well after the fact, and then every once in a while, it's right in their face, and they can praise God as it happens."

"Can I ask you something?"

"Anything."

"You said once you almost were allowed to go check on Christy for a quick visit. When was that?"

"The Master and I had been checking on Christy as stress at her job in Alabama had gotten very tense, and he was concerned. He had let me know of the accident and to be on standby in case I was needed and in case the whole team needed to be notified if it got real bad."

"What do you mean?"

"Well, surgery can sometimes be tricky, and her surgery was over ten hours long. This was a very quiet house for a couple of days."

"I guess it was a good thing at the time that I did not understand what was going on. It was at that time I had to quit sleeping on the foot of the bed with her."

"Wait a minute. She let you sleep on the bed with her, as big as you are?"

"Yea," he said in quiet remembrance. "It had been nice, but she had all this equipment attached to her bed after the accident to keep her arm in constant motion even when sleeping. Those first few weeks after surgery, she was probably was in bed more than out of bed. I remember Mary buying a baby monitor so that she could hear Christy if needed."

"Her body went through a lot, and it needed to heal. Sometimes, sleep is the best thing."

"But she healed well. I remember her saying the doctor called her the star patient. She even used her as an example once with a young patient who was feeling sorry for himself. She told that young guy it would be a shame if a fifty-year-old woman could beat him at arm wrestling so that he better do his exercises."

"That sounds like something she would do." Ruth chuckled.

"Hey guys," said Spot as he and the remaining team members along with another new cook brought breakfast. "This is Emily, and she is a pastry specialist."

"And it smells fantastic," stated Sam.

"Nothing real special, guys," said Emily. "Cheese-filled Danish with fresh fruit."

"Thank you for bringing it down to us," said Ruth.

"It was on my way out. I am headed over to the final planning meeting for the big cook-off."

"That is going to be so fun. I heard that maybe Abraham or even Noah may be there for the story time," said Spot. "Thanks again, Emily, and have a good meeting."

After heads were bowed for thanks, they enjoyed the quiet of the day as they ate their pastries.

"Dittims, you ready to resume?"

"Sure. I think you all know that Christy was not real happy with work. She wanted to find something less stressful and was also tired of triple-digit temperatures for four months out of the year. I remember her telling Mary that she probably was not going to get on anywhere due to her age, but she was going to look anyway and see. About six months after coming back from her accident, she stared getting calls from a company that had plants in several states. They needed a quality manager in two separate plants on opposite sides of the country, so Christy went to interview with them both. After a few months of interviewing and waiting, she was offered the job at either facility, and she accepted the facility in Iowa. There was a dear family friend that lived in Green Bay and was familiar with the area of where this plant was located. She told Christy she thought she would enjoy the Midwest and that the area, while small, had a good report of being a good place to live. So a renter was found for their house, a rental house for them in Iowa was found, and off we went. Mary had Lakota and the cats, and I rode in the front seat with Christy. She had packed stuff in the floor board, then covered it with a blanket, giving me a platform to lie on. Mary had her special items she refused to put in the moving van, and Christy place the yard work stuff and potted plants in the back of the pickup truck. The moving van had the majority of their things including all the furniture but gave them only two days to get to the rental house in Iowa, which was over a thousand miles. Christy was funny. At the first part of the trip, she would state a hundred miles down nine hundred plus to go, two hundred down eight hundred plus to go. When they would cross a state line, she would stop and take a picture of each state sign, except for Iowa because that was on the bridge railing when they crossed the Mississippi River. That's a big bridge."

"And that is not even the widest part of the river?" stated Spot.

"No, but it is the point where the river turns west before returning south again. When we would go on sightseeing rides, we always took the highway that meandered right by the river's edge. It was really pretty area."

"I remember the rides we would take along the rivers in Florida," commented Sam. "Christy would drive through all the small communities close to where their summer house was.

"There is something peaceful about water in rivers and ponds, even oceans with their waves crashing on the beach," mused Ruth.

"I think some of my favorite exploring walks in Illinois were in the Chippiannock Historical Cemetery. That area of the country had been the home of the Sauk Indian tribes. So the name of the cemetery carries an Indian name meaning 'place of the dead.' It has rolling hills filled with large oak trees and firs that kept most the entire area in shade. It isn't very large, making it a perfect place for quiet reflection. We would see other people waking there as well, some with pets and some just by themselves. Christy even made friends with those she would see often when we walked there."

"Was it near the river?" asked Nellie.

"No, but I bet in its early years before the trees got big, you could see the river from the tops of some of the hills. It was established in the 1850s."

"What else did you do there?" asked Ruth.

"I have heard several of you speak against fireworks, but they would do it differently. The fireworks in the area were shot off barges in the middle of the river. There were several bridges that crossed the river, so we would go to the bridge on the west side of town because its rise was higher than town and it had parking areas on the side of it. You could see the fireworks without being in the crowd of people. Plus you were far enough away where the sound was not that bad."

"I might have enjoyed that," said Ruth as several nodded in approval.

OUR HOME OF LOVE

"That did not include the lack of peacefulness in our neighborhood, though. A few weeks before and after the event on the river, people were shooting off smaller fireworks until late in the evening. That was most annoying. Even though I could not really hear it, the vibrations in the older house we were living in could be felt with those sound vibrations. I stayed on the couch so I would not feel them as easily as on the wooden floor."

"Boys!" said Gypsy.

"Excuse me," probed Ruth.

"Boys, think about it. It is just that way in Christy family and even our Love Team. Both of Christy's boys played with fire, evidently on more than one occasion. John played with firecrackers, and you guys, excluding Spot of course, think loud noises and risky business is fun."

"Well, it's not all of us," defended Zero, "but we are probably more curious about how things work, where you ladies are more into caring and nurturing than us guys."

"And there is a divine purpose to that truth, even in the animal kingdom," came a voice from behind them.

Everyone's head snapped in the direction of the voice and saw the Master approach and settle onto one of the benches with them.

"You see," he continued, "in the beginning, man was created for the purpose to care for the animals and the garden that were created before him, but he needed a helpmate, so then I created woman as a helpmate. And, Ruth, as I have heard you explain on more than one occasion, no one creation is more important than the other. I created all things for my purpose, none more important than the other and with each having their own gifts to further what I need them to do, even with you animals. Remember the old stories of war and takeover where I told my chosen ones to take over the land. It was men who went to fight. They are built different than women and have a different purpose. Women came from man as a helper and nurturer for the family. Woman has to be strong in her own way to be able to do that. Now I am not saying women can't be fighters in war time, because I have some strong women on my team, but I want you to see the general purpose between male and female. Look at the animal world.

Generally, the males are larger in their own breed and usually stronger, but the females are faster and more agile. Here is a good example from your Love Team. Your smallest member is Sandra. How many times has she beaten you guys during Maze Race Days?"

They all looked at each other and nodded this was indeed true.

"Let's look at the other side of the size comparison. Gracie and Azer same breed similar size, but Azer's structure is taller broader through the shoulders, and his personality is ready for any energy-related task I ask him. Gracie is more reserved and thinks more about the task at hand. She is more organized and has leader potential. I am not saying that Azer does not have the same leader potential, but I need his energy and daredevil traits for a whole different purpose. As you all know, Ruth is the lead canine for this house and Love Team and is more in tuned with what my goals are for this group and the final banquet. So I have a question for the rest of you. Who knows what the difference is between pulling the carts to help others like you guys did the other day and Sandra's quick agility when she is running the race at Maze Day?"

Everyone looked lost as they pondered his question.

"Well," said Dittims, "pulling is a task to help others but running is just fun?"

The Master smiled, liking Dittims's answer.

"That is a good observation, Dittims, but not the correct answer I am looking for."

"How about one is teamwork and one is not?" suggested Azer.

"Another good answer, but not what I am looking for."

"Does it have anything to do with speed or strength," asked Gypsy.

"No. Any other guesses?" he asked when it got quiet for a moment.

"I think we are a bit lost," said Spot.

"Not really, you are all thinking too hard. The game days we have are geared for each animal and person's abilities to hone and strengthen those abilities. It's training. Everything we do here is training for the last fight, whether it involves speed, strength, finesse, creativeness, organization, or any other gift I have given you for you to help me and my kingdom regardless of how very small a task you may feel it is. It will be important. I told my disciples the importance of the entire body that no part is more important than the other. You guys have four legs. Think how difficult it would be with three. All members of the body are important to work together, whether the body is a single person or animal or a team. Therefore, the entire Love Team needs to work together as a unit. Then it will combine with other love teams in other houses, other areas, and so on so that the entire heavens work together as one entity. You are all, man and beast alike, in training individually with specific task that I give you. Then you are training together to work together as a team to facilitate events, nurture others not in your group, and just learn to do my will. And you all are doing well, but there is still a lot more to train for so keep going. Ask Ruth for guidance as you train, and of course, you can always, always ask me. Just remember the goal."

"So, Dittims," he said as he looked at Dittims, seeing his face filling with fear and wonder at the same time.

"No need to be fearful. You are doing fine, but I think it is time for some one on one with me."

"Okay. What do you need?"

"First," he said as he chuckled coming to love on Dittims, "I need you to relax. I want to tell you all what I see in you and what my plan for you is. Let's you and I go for a walk in the maze and enjoy the garden together."

As they walk up the hill toward the maze, a quiet hush fell over the group.

"I remember when he and I had the walk through the maze," said Ruth. "I was very surprised of the love and tenderness, although I had heard the many stories Christy had read. Feeling it firsthand really can't be explained without you having the experience."

"I think it is also different for each one of us," said Sam. "I just know I would never think of myself the way the he thinks of me and of his plan for me and his love. How can you not understand his love?"

"Well, the father of lies still has a strong hold on man while they are still on Earth," said Ruth. "And it is our duty to not only learn all we can here but to always be in prayerful mindset for our loved ones still in his clutched hands. I remember a plaque Christy had on her wall in the living room saying, "I would rather live my life believing there is a loving God that watches over me and die finding out that there wasn't, than to live my life believing there is no loving God and die to find out there was and missed out on everything.'

Epilogue

"Tell me, Dittims," asked the Master as they settled on a bench in the garden, "how are you feeling about this place?"

"It's amazing. I feel so renewed and loved. Not that I didn't feel loved before, it's just different."

"How are you doing in the team?"

"I am not sure what you are asking me? The team is awesome. They are teaching me so much about here and about others here and how to help. It's amazing the teamwork here and how everyone works together to complete a task or project."

"How do you think the team feels about you?"

"Okay, I guess. Everyone seems to like me."

The Master chuckled as Dittims looked perplexed at his questioning.

"Am I missing something?" asked Dittims.

"Not really. Your humbleness will serve you well, but I want you to understand your own strengths and leadership abilities as well. I am going to put you more in training with Spot and Jake, and Ruth as well. Listen to them. They have already told me about the strength that they see in you. I want you to see it, own it, and learn to use it. I have a specific mission for you that I am sure you will do very well in once you get where I need you to be. You are a member of one of a large canine love teams, one of the larger ones in this division. In these larger teams, there is a hierarchy leadership responsibility. What that means is I have established multiple leaders in those teams for specific purposes. For example, Ruth is the nurturing and care leader of this team. Gracie has leadership over tasks and projects due to her organization way of thinking. Sandra is a leader on quick things that need to be done in a quick manner. All members have leadership due to their strengths and process abilities. Due to your disabilities on earth, you do not understand your strengths so I am training you to get ready for Mimi."

"I don't understand."

"I know, but you will. Once we get you assured of who you are and you own your capabilities, you will be ready to train Mimi when she gets here. You and Mimi will be the protectors for this team and house. Now protection has an entirely different meaning here from what Mimi understand as protection, and I will need you to train her of the difference. She already has the guard dog protective attributes, but they will need to be fine-tuned for here, and I will want you to show her how. Your humble nature combined with your strength of character will make you a force to be reckoned with, and you will make a formidable trainer for my kingdom. Once you both have the training perfected, you will join other protective teams around this kingdom on the final day of battle."

"You think I can be all that?"

"I know you can. I know all of my creation's abilities as I gave them gifts for my purpose. Let's do it together."

"Okay, I'm in."

*****

OUR HOME OF LOVE

Baby Ruth
Dittims
Dittims Travels to Iowa
Me Sitting on Spot
Gypsy and Blacky
Azer
Mimi
Samantha (Sam)
Lakota
Zero

About the Author

Anita Neal is a retired quality manager originally from Valdosta, Georgia, but currently living in Rock Island, Illinois. Her love of animals and people inspire her writing through her books, her short stories, and her poetry. Her main emphasis in all that she does and tries to accomplish through her blog is to always be kind. Her current canine companion is Mimi, a black lab and black-and-tan coon hound mix who is mostly in protection mode unless asleep on her back on the couch.

CPSIA information can be obtained
at www.ICGtesting.com
Printed in the USA
FSHW020238161119
64078FS